Paul Hutchens

MOODY PRESS
CHICAGO

Revised Edition, 1998

Original Title: *White Boat Rescue at Sugar Creek*

ISBN: 0-8024-7030-0

1 3 5 7 9 10 8 6 4 2

Printed in the United States of America

PREFACE

Hi—from a member of the Sugar Creek Gang!

It's just that I don't know which one I am. When I was good, I was Little Jim. When I did bad things—well, sometimes I was Bill Collins or even mischievous Poetry.

You see, I am the daughter of Paul Hutchens, and I spent many an hour listening to him read his manuscript as far as he had written it that particular day. I went along to the north woods of Minnesota, to Colorado, and to the various other places he would go to find something different for the Gang to do.

Now the years have passed—more than fifty, actually. My father is in heaven, but the Gang goes on. All thirty-six books are still in print and now are being updated for today's readers with input from my five children, who also span the decades from the '50s to the '70s.

The real Sugar Creek is in Indiana, and my father and his six brothers were the original Gang. But the idea of the books and their ministry were and are the Lord's. It is He who keeps the Gang going.

PAULINE HUTCHENS WILSON

1

It was one of the finest summer mornings I had ever seen, I thought as I rolled over and out of bed, took a deep breath of fresh air, and looked out the open window of my upstairs room.

The June sun was already up, shooting long slants of light across the backyard and garden. Old Red Addie, our big red mother hog, was grunting around the front door of her apartment hog house at the south end of her pen. Fifteen or twenty of Mom's happy laying hens were already up and scratching near the garden gate, scratching and eating and singing and scratching and eating—gobbling down what Dad calls "grains, greens, grubs, and grits," which is the variety of food a good laying hen has to have to stay well and lay an egg a day.

I guess there's nothing in the world that looks finer to a boy than an outdoor morning when there is plenty of open space for the sunshine to fall in and when the sky itself is as clear and blue as the water in Sugar Creek looks on a clear day when you are looking down at it from the bridge.

In the field east of the barn, the corn was talking in a thousand voices, making a husky, rusty rustling sound, as it says in a certain poem we had to memorize in school.

I started shoving myself into my jeans to make a dash downstairs and see if Mom's pancakes and bacon would taste as good as they smelled. Suddenly, from somewhere beyond the twin pignut trees at the north end of the garden, there came a meadowlark's juicy-noted, half-wild, very musical, rippling song. It seemed to say, "Summer is coming and springtime is *here!*"

But a beautiful, wonderful outdoor summer was already here, having the time of its life making corn and beans and potatoes grow, making birds build nests to raise their baby birds in, spreading blankets of wildflowers all over Sugar Creek territory, and even making the fish bite.

Downstairs, Mom had the radio tuned to a favorite program whose theme song was "Every Day's a Wonderful Day."

Before I started to make my usual race for the head of the stairs, I happened to see our big *Webster's Unabridged Dictionary* in the alcove by the bookcase. I decided to quickly look up a word—any word my eye happened to land on—which would be my word for the day. That was one of our family's fun games for the summer. Each person selected a new word from the dictionary, and all of us used it over and over again at different times during the day, just to get acquainted with it.

Already that summer I'd learned important words such as *leisure,* which Dad said was pronounced with a long *e,* but Mom said she liked a short *e* better. It meant "spare time," which a boy hardly ever has enough of. I also learned a new meaning for the word *freeze,* which is what a gopher or chipmunk or groundhog does when it is startled or scared. It rears up on its haunches to study and think and wait until it seems safe for it to drop down to the ground and go on about its business.

I quickly ran my right forefinger and both eyes down a column of words under the letter *f* and stopped when I came to a word I thought was new. It was "flotsam." I didn't even dream what an important word it was going to be before the day was over—and especially before the summer came to its exciting and dangerous climax.

On the way downstairs I was saying over to myself the dictionary's definition of "flotsam," which was "goods cast or swept from a vessel into the sea and found floating."

Before I reached the bottom step, my imagination had me drifting along out in a boat in Sugar Creek. And one of the gang accidentally or on purpose was rocking the boat. Then the boat capsized, and all of us were getting spilled out into what my mind's eye saw was a wild, stormy, sealike creek. Our oars fell overboard, and the waves carried them away. Fishing tackle boxes, bait canteens, straw hats—everything was turned into flotsam.

That was as far as my shipwreck got right then because I was near enough to the kitchen table to make a dive for my chair and start sawing away on a stack of pancakes.

For some reason, though, I didn't sit down right away. I got to go out to the barn first to help my father finish the chores, which meant the horses and cattle got to eat their breakfast before we did.

At the table, Mom's wonderful day was interrupted by Charlotte Ann's upsetting her bowl of cereal in her high chair tray, making flotsam out of it in several milk-spattered directions. Some of it landed on the island shore of Mom's brown linoleum floor. Mom scolded her gently.

"You won't believe it," I said to my family, as I denied myself wanting to sit still and let Mom mop up the mess, "but my word for the day is 'flotsam.'"

"I believe it," Mom said, trying to keep her excitement in her mind. "Every day's not only a wonderful day, but it nearly always has a lot of little upsets, and the main boat upsetters in this house are my two wonderful children. One of them not only rocks the boat and often upsets it but actually throws her goods overboard."

Dad, maybe trying to lighten our family boat a little, said, "There are three words that usually go together: 'flotsam,' 'jetsam,' and 'lagan.' Lagan, Son, if you ever look up its meaning, is goods cast to drift or sometimes sunk on purpose, but it's attached to a buoy to float, so that if anybody finds it, they will know it belongs to *somebody*."

Trying to be funny and maybe not being very, I managed to say, "Who would want to tie anything to a *boy?*"

"B-U-O-Y," Dad spelled and winked at Mom. Then he remarked to her, "Anything tied to a B-O-Y would be *really* sunk—some other father's boy, of course."

Well, we had a few minutes' talk about a Bible verse, which we try to do once a day at our house so that we would have an anchor to tie our minds to in case we had an upset of some kind. Then we left the table and moved out into the working part of the day, hoping it would be as wonderful *all* day as it had been up to now—which it had to be for a certain B-O-Y.

I say it *had* to be, because the six sets of parents of the Sugar Creek Gang were sending the whole gang on a special errand, which I will tell you about in a few minutes, just as soon as I can write that far.

"Here's a little flotsam," Mom said, stopping me as I was about to go outdoors. She handed me a little basket containing a warm package of something wrapped in transparent plastic. It smelled as if it had just come from the oven, which it had. "Be sure, now, to make the Fenwicks welcome. Remember your best manners; smile and offer to do anything you see needing to be done."

"I will," I said, enjoying the smell of the warm, freshly baked something or other.

And away I went, remembering my best manners even at home by shutting the screen door quietly. I was quickly on my way down to the Black Widow Stump to meet the gang. As soon as the whole gang was there, we'd have a hurry-up meeting to decide different things. Then we'd all take whatever our different mothers had baked and go across the bridge and down the creek to the Maple Leaf, a brand-new cabin we had helped build on a wooded knoll across the creek from the mouth of the branch.

In the Maple Leaf, having moved in only yesterday, was a missionary couple. They were to be the very first missionaries to spend part of their furlough in it. Dr. John Fenwick and his wife, Elona, had spent a lot of years in Central America, and they had come home for a rest and to get a little change from the very hot, humid climate that far south.

John Fenwick was a medical doctor, we found out, and *his* doctor down in Costa Rica had ordered him home for a rest. He had the kind of heart trouble called "angina pectoris."

The Maple Leaf, maybe I ought to tell you, was built on property owned by Old Man Paddler, the kind, long-whiskered old man who lived up in the hills and was always doing kind things for people—especially for missionaries, whom he seemed to like almost better than he did boys.

The wooded knoll had been given to the Sugar Creek Church, and all the men of the church as well as a lot of other men in the neighborhood—and also the Sugar Creek Gang itself—had built the cabin for free. That had seemed even more fun than swimming and diving in the old swimming hole or catching sunfish and goggle-eyes. It certainly was a lot more enjoyment than weeding the garden and helping clean out the barn.

Anyway, today was *the* day. As soon as we'd get our welcoming visit over, the rest of the whole morning would be ours to do with as we liked, our twelve parents had told us.

Mom's final orders about politeness having been tossed back into the history section of my mind, I was now on my way like a "barefoot boy with cheek of tan," as a poem by James Whitcomb Riley says. I sped across the yard to the walnut tree by the gate, gave the rope swing a fling toward the east, and leaped out of the way when its heavy board seat came swooshing back. It would have bowled me over if it had hit me.

I took a quick look around the base of the tree to see if there were any new ant lion larva traps, and there were—three new conical pits in the powdery sand. I knew that buried at the bottom of each pit—now seven all together—was a hairy larva, the hatched egg of a night-flying insect. Each larva would stay buried, all except its head, until an ant or other insect accidentally tumbled into its trap. And then, *wham! Flurry! Chop! Chop! Slurp! Slurp!* And the ant lion would have had its breakfast without having to work for it or wait for its mother to cook it.

Any boy who knows anything about an ant

lion knows that its mother is a damselfly and that she lays her eggs on the surface of sandy or dusty soil under a rocky ledge or close to a house or barn or tree. As soon as the wormlike babies are born, they dig those cone-shaped traps themselves and are ready for breakfast without having to dress or help their parents do the chores or wash dishes or baby-sit, since each ant lion is its own baby-sitter.

But also, an ant lion never knows how good it feels to plop-plop across a dusty road with its bare feet—which it doesn't have anyway—or go racing like the wind through the woods on the way to meet a gang of other ant lions its age and size.

I must have daydreamed several minutes too long at the walnut tree, because from the house I heard Mom yell, "Hurry up, Bill, and get gone! Charlotte Ann's on the warpath! She wants to go with you. So the sooner you're out of sight, the sooner you'll be out of her mind, and she'll be out of my hair!"

The worry in Mom's voice made me sing out across the grassy yard to her, "Every day's a wonderful day!"

"For B-O-Y-S!" she called back. "Now you hurry up. And tell the Fenwicks we're glad they're here and to let us know whenever there's anything we can do for them. Be sure to make them feel at home!"

And then away I did go, plop-plopping my bare feet in the dust all the way across the road. I hadn't any sooner swung up and over the rail fence than I remembered that at that very place, a few yards from the elderberry bushes, I had had a fierce, fast fistfight with one of the orneriest boys that ever lived in the territory. That boy's name was Shorty Long. In spite of my having given him a licking, he was still one of the worst boys anywhere around.

The only peace the gang had from him was when his family was away spending their winter vacations in a warm climate somewhere, which they did every year.

I took a look at the arena where we'd had our battle and said, gritting my teeth, "Take that—and that—and *that!*" I swung my one free fist around a little, then came to myself and started on toward the Black Widow Stump, saying to myself as I ran—and quoting my father, who had given me a talking to about keeping my temper under control—"Tempers are given to us by the Lord, Son. You can use them or lose them. If you waste your good temper in an explosion, you feel *sick* afterward. Some people actually feel as weak as a sick cat."

"How," I had asked my lowered-eyebrowed father that day—he had his own temper under good control at the time—"how can a boy who has had his nose bashed in a battle *keep* from losing his temper?"

Dad's answer was as if I had thrown a hard snowball at him and he had dodged it. Here is part of what he told me: "Just keep your eye on your mother. A hundred times a day things go wrong around the house and farm that could make her the saddest or maddest person in the world. Instead, she keeps her mind filled with thoughts of God and with Bible truth. She keeps her heart's radio tuned to heaven and—well, you just watch her, and you'll see!"

I *had* been watching my wonderful gray-brown-haired mother ever since, and little by little I was learning.

"But," I said to myself as I zip-zip-zipped and zag-zag-zagged my way along on the little brown path to the Black Widow Stump, "What do I do today if my worst enemy happens along and stirs my temper all up with something he says or does?"

Shorty Long, being the only boy in the neighborhood whose parents took winter vacations in warm climates, was very proud of himself and very uppity about things they saw and did in the places they visited.

I gave my shoulders a twisting shrug as if I was a bucking bronco in a rodeo. And right away, in my mind, I *was* a bucking bronco, and Shorty Long was a cowboy trying to ride me and couldn't. I was a trained Western pony, my mane blowing in the wind. Shorty Long was lying in the dust behind me as I leaped into a fast gallop toward what was maybe going to be one of the most wonderful days the gang would ever have.

Maybe.

2

It was one of the happiest gallops through the woods I'd ever had. Nature helped me feel excited by letting me scare up a cottontail rabbit, whose white almost-no-tail went bob-bob-bobbing along toward a brush pile near a patch of light green mayapples.

"Don't worry, Little Brer Rabbit!" I called after him. "I know you were born and bred in the bramble patch, and I wouldn't hurt you for anything in the world!"

While I was still stopped, I eased over to a little thicket of seven-foot-tall bushes. I wanted to have a look at a thrush's nest I'd stopped at yesterday, to see if any of the four green-and-brown speckled eggs had hatched. And I got one of the worst scoldings that ever a boy can get. The mother thrush came storming out of those bushes, leaping from one branch to another, saying *"Prut-prut!"* in a short, sharp, angry, high-pitched tone. It certainly didn't sound anything like her early spring song, which is one of the sweetest bird melodies in the whole territory.

I worked my way cautiously through the branches and took a quick peek into the nest, but there weren't any baby birds. There were still only the same four light green, thickly speckled eggs. Then I stepped back and got out of the way, because suddenly *two* rusty red birds were storming all around, screaming at me as if I wasn't a part of nature at all.

"All right! All right!" I scolded them back. "What're you doing up there, letting your eggs get cold! Get back on the nest! And learn to keep your voices down when you have company!"

I wasn't really angry at them, though. I was remembering what Mom once told me about the brown thrasher, which is another name for the brown thrush. She had said, "It sings best in late April and May. But when it begins to build its nest and get its family started, it's too busy looking after the house and the children."

I took a good-bye look at the half-hidden nest of grapevine tendrils, dead grass, twigs, and stringlike roots, and said to the eggs, "Now you hurry up and get yourselves hatched! And furthermore, from the day you're old enough to know anything, start being polite to strangers! Obey your parents and make it easy for your mother to sing around the house!"

With that advice, I swung back into the path made by boys' bare feet, listening in my mind to the words of a song we use every Sunday or so in our church school. It starts, "Look all around you, find someone in need. Help somebody today!"

That, Bill Collins, I explained to myself, *is the real reason why you feel fine inside this morning. You're on the way to do something for somebody else—not just to have fun for yourself.*

"You're right," I answered me and galloped on.

At the bottom of the slope, maybe fifty feet from the Black Widow Stump, I stopped again and looked through the dancing heat waves hanging over the open space to see if any of the gang was already there, but none of them was.

Listening for footsteps, I heard instead the busy buzzing of maybe seven thousand honeybees, which this time of year went swimming and diving and tumbling over each other among the flowers of the leaning linden tree. At the same time, my nose was caught up into a whirlwind of the sweetest natural perfume in the whole territory—the nectarlike scent of thousands of creamy yellow flowers of the tree that bees seem to like even better than they do wild crab apple blossoms.

"Slaves," I said, half to myself and half to the bees, "you don't know it, but you're working for my father. The honey you make out of that sweet nectar is being stored in my father's own beehives. But we do appreciate it very much, my little friends. Maybe that's the reason you're so happy—*you're* helping somebody else, even if you don't know it!"

Sitting on his haunches on the stump was one of my favorite animal brothers, a chestnut brown chipmunk. He was looking the world over, listening to see if there was any danger.

"Good morning, Chippy-chip-chee!" I cooed, not wanting to scare him. The second he was scared, he would all of a sudden disappear the way other ground squirrels do. Sometimes—but only sometimes—Chippy-chip-chee would let us creep up really close. Then, maybe deciding we were for sure his friends, he would scoot back and forth all around in front of us, working his way closer and closer until he got up enough nerve to dash in and pick up a nut or piece of bread or cracker crumb we had tossed out to him.

For some reason Chippy was a little nervous today. And when he saw me creeping toward him, like a flash he was gone.

Getting to the Black Widow Stump before any of the rest of the gang arrived, I plopped myself down in the long, brown, last year's grass to rest, not being as tired as I would have been if I had been pushing our one-row cultivator across Theodore Collins's garden.

My nose was close to the flotsam Mom had given me, and I wondered if it would taste as good as it smelled. Right then it seemed like a good idea to put it about three feet behind me, which I did.

And right away I was daydreaming again—this time while I was looking toward the linden tree and the rail fence beside it. Growing there, and dancing a little in the breeze, were maybe seventeen yellowish fawn lilies, nodding their heads to each other as fawn lilies do when they are in full bloom.

I was jarred out of my daydream right then by a flock of voices. Rolling over and up to a sitting position, I leaned back against the stump and watched five different-sized, different-shaped boys moving toward me. There was Big Jim, our leader, the oldest and biggest of us, the only one with fuzz on his upper lip and whose voice was beginning to sound like the quawking of the big night heron that lives in the swamp. There was Circus, our acrobat, who had six sisters and never got a chance to help his mother with the dishes—which is why Charlotte Ann ought to hurry and grow up. There was Little Jim, carrying—as he always does—his handmade ash cane. There was Dragonfly, the most spindly-legged one of us, and last of all, Poetry, my almost best friend, the chubbiest one of us. He was on a diet this summer and *had* been on it on and off all spring.

In the right or left hand of each boy was a package of something for the Fenwicks.

Almost right away we called our business meeting to order so that we could decide different things we would try to do the next few weeks to make the Fenwicks feel at home. In the middle of the meeting, Big Jim unfolded a piece of typewriter paper, saying, "Here, gang, is something we can do this morning."

On the paper was a hand-drawn map of the whole Sugar Creek playground. Outlined on the page were the spring at the bottom of the incline, the swimming hole, the bridge, the island, the cave, Old Man Paddler's cabin up in the hills, the haunted house, Old Tom the

Trapper's canine cemetery behind it, the best fishing places—things like that.

Our meeting over, we were soon on our way, all of us having put our flotsam in the big picnic basket Poetry had brought his in—and letting him carry it. A vote we had just taken had decided it that way.

Pretty soon we came to the rail fence near the bridge and went through or over or under the rails, whichever our minds told us to do. Then we started across the board-floored, extra-long bridge. It is over one of the widest places in Sugar Creek and has several deep fishing holes below it. The best fishing place is on the north shore, fifteen feet out from the leaning sycamore tree.

Halfway across, we stopped, all of us facing west to look toward the island and especially toward the wooded knoll where the Maple Leaf missionary cabin was. Blue wood smoke was rising from the barbecue pit.

"Look, g–ang!" Dragonfly beside me stammered. "There–there–there's a white boat at the dock!"

I'd already seen it. With its prow moored to the dock post was what looked like a brand-new, shining aluminum boat.

"And–and–and," Dragonfly stammered on, "it's got a life preserver! Who needs a life preserver around here?"

Big Jim answered in a teacher voice, "Every boat ought to have one, even in a creek like ours. There are a lot of places too deep for wading. And besides, you could accidentally gulp water in an upset and not be able to swim. You can drown in a bathtub, you know. A boy nearly did last week in Brown County—remember?"

"The boat's got a name on its side," Little Jim said.

I tried to read the letters but couldn't make them out, and neither could any of us.

Anyway, it was time to go on, which we kind of bashfully did. Not a one of us had seen the Fenwicks in person. We had only seen their pictures on the bulletin board in the foyer of the Sugar Creek Church. We'd seen and heard quite a few different missionaries in our church but had never had a chance to see how they lived in the ordinary everyday world. For the next few weeks, we would get to, beginning just seven minutes from now.

Pretty soon we were all the way across the bridge and down the steep embankment on the other side, walking single file on the path that bordered the shore, not hurrying, because maybe we wouldn't be able to act natural when we got there.

Back at the Black Widow Stump we had voted for Poetry to be the spokesman, knock at the Maple Leaf door, and hand in the basket of baked things. Big Jim had ordered, "After that, everybody act natural. Just be ourselves."

But *that* wouldn't be easy, my mind told me as I dodged the swinging branch of a willow Dragonfly hadn't bothered to hold back. If I acted natural right that very second, a spindly-legged boy would get tripped by the right foot of the red-haired boy behind him. Then, if we both kept on acting natural, there'd be a rough-and-tumble scramble of arms and legs, plus some grunts and maybe even a few groans.

Also, how can a boy act natural just because he has been ordered to or voted to? Especially when, at a time like this, it would be unnatural to act natural.

At the pier that we had helped our fathers make, we stopped to study the white boat and to admire the outboard motor attached to the stern. Just looking at that very pretty shining new boat made our own boat, which was chained to a small maple sapling up near the spring, seem like a last year's bird's nest. Ours was made of wood. It needed painting and also cleaning on the inside.

We were still standing at the dock, admiring the boat, feeling a little envious of it maybe and *not* liking ours as well as we usually did, when John Fenwick came down to where we were. He was panting a little, being short of breath as if he had seen and heard us and had come in a hurry to make us welcome.

While he was still coming, Poetry gave a low whistle in my ear and whispered, "Look at those bulging muscles!"

The gray-brown-haired missionary, still working his way down the slope, was dressed in gray everyday slacks and an almost snow-white T-shirt. His face, arms, neck, and shoulders were a healthy tan, and their muscles did look like the muscles of the village blacksmith in a school poem of that name, part of which goes:

> Under a spreading chestnut tree
> The village smithy stands;
> . . . .
> And the muscles of his brawny arms
> Are strong as iron bands.

Poetry, who is always thinking in rhyme, having maybe a hundred-and-one poems stored in what he calls the "reference section" of his mind, whispered to me a little more about "The Village Blacksmith."

> "He goes on Sunday to the church,
> And sits among his boys;
> He hears the parson pray and preach;
> He hears his daughter's voice . . ."

I don't know what I expected a missionary dressed in ordinary clothes to look like, but for some reason it felt good to see John Fenwick looking and acting as much like a human being as a human being does.

Anyway, we pretty soon found out that the Guenther Longs had spent their winter vacation in Costa Rica, and on Sundays they had attended the little mission chapel there. Then the Fenwicks found out that the Longs lived at Sugar Creek, and the Longs found out that the Fenwicks had been invited to spend a month of their furlough in the new Sugar Creek missionary cabin.

"Well," John Fenwick told us, "that's why I bought the new boat. When I was a boy, our family lived for several years on a beautiful little creek like this one. And the only boat I had was a battered old homemade one that leaked like a sieve. So I thought that for once in my life I'd like one that would help me live my boyhood dreams in a modern sort of way. Here, let me show you the very latest in boats."

The big missionary stepped out onto the dock, asking us to follow him, and that's when we got a close-up of the long, wide, aluminum boat.

"The seats," John explained, stooping and showing us, "have built-in Styrofoam, which makes it impossible for the boat to sink. That's another thing about my boyhood boat—I had an upset with it once, and it sank. It wouldn't even float to shore.

"You boys remember that, if you're ever out on a large body of water in a modern boat—*never* try to swim to shore if it's far. Just stay with the boat. Most of them will not sink unless they have too much weight in them and too much water. Usually you can hang on outside the boat, keeping your body under—all except your head, of course—and by and by your boat will drift to a shore or island or somewhere."

While John Fenwick was still talking and admiring his boat, looking at it as though he was a boy of our age and size again, I had my mind on a certain other boat that I knew would sink if it accidentally got filled with water, especially if it had a boy or two in it or even hanging onto it. It seemed maybe there wasn't a boat in the world that was as worthless as ours, which *didn't* have two new lightweight oars, two metal carrying handles on its stern, a self-bailing assembly, a fish stringer ring, or any of what John called "foam flotation encased in its seats."

Dragonfly, who had never liked our old boat anyway—because sometimes, especially in ragweed season, he thought it was the wet wood of the gunwales that made him sneeze—right then sneaked an idea into my mind. He said, "If we'd make him a member of the gang while he is here, he might let us borrow his boat."

"Sh!" Big Jim, who had seen us whispering, stopped us with a shush, because right that minute John's wife was standing at the top of the incline by the large wide-topped stump of a tree one of our Sugar Creek fathers had cut down.

She was calling to us, "Come on up!"

We went on up, and Elona Fenwick was maybe even more like a human being than her husband was. She had a very cheerful sense of humor, and she looked at us with her twinkling brown eyes as though she liked barefoot boys with dusty feet and everyday play clothes.

3

But that wasn't all Elona Fenwick seemed to like. We found that out a little later when she surprised us by saying, "The Longs are such wonderful people, and their boy—Shorty, they sometimes call him—is so polite. Any parent would be thankful to have a boy like that."

I must have been staring my astonishment, because right then Poetry eased an elbow into my ribs as he whispered, "Don't look so surprised!"

From where we were standing we could read the lettering on the prow of the boat now, and it was some kind of foreign name: V-I-D-A E-T-E-R-N-A.

"That's Spanish for 'Life Eternal,'" Elona explained when she heard Little Jim spelling out the letters. "The children in the Costa Rica mission school sing, *'Yo tengo vida eterna en mi corazon.'* That means, 'I have eternal life in my heart.'"

We were all acting natural without realizing it, it seemed. It was easy to chatter along, especially when the Fenwicks were making us feel at home even more than we were them.

"I suppose Shorty belongs to your club," Mrs. Fenwick said. "He didn't say so, but he seemed such a polite boy, it would just be natural for him to."

We were sitting in the shade of the big maple tree then, having to drink a cup apiece of some kind of homemade fruit drink she called Costa Rican punch. We were also eating a cookie apiece out of the flotsam basket.

How could we tell them that Shorty Long *wasn't* a member of the gang because he didn't want to be and also because *we* didn't want him to be? That he was a filthy talker and sometimes said things that, as my father once expressed it, "are not fit to be poured down into a city sewer!"

Also—and maybe most important of all—we couldn't let a boy like that pal around with us unless he could learn to talk respectfully about girls. That is why I had had the fierce, fast fistfight with him beside the elderberry bushes across the gravel road from "Theodore Collins" on our mailbox. It was especially something he had said about Lucille Browne, Circus's ordinary-looking sister, who sometimes smiles at me across the schoolroom and who can knock a home run and kill a spider or a snake without batting an eye.

After the cookies, Big Jim unfolded his homemade map, spread it out on the flat surface of the stump, and began to point out to the Fenwicks the places of special interest.

"Here, beginning at the mouth of the branch—over there by the big pine tree—is the path that leads to the sycamore tree near the entrance of the cave. And right here is the trail leading into the swamp and onto the muskrat pond. On your left, as you walk along a ways is the beginning of the quagmire and the quicksand. There's a barbed-wire fence and a sign to warn you—"

Dragonfly put in a few stammering words right there, saying, "One n–n–night we saw old John Till's head lying out there right in the middle of it. Its eyes were open, and its voice was calling, 'H–h–h–help!'"

John Fenwick looked from the map to Dragonfly's pinched, mischievous little face and said, "You're kidding!"

"It was John Till himself," Big Jim explained. "He had been drinking and strayed off the path and had sunk all the way down to his chin. There was a rock down there, and he was standing on it and struggling to keep from sliding off into still deeper mire—"

"And–and we saved him," Dragonfly said proudly.

"The grace of God," John Fenwick said. "He used you boys to rescue him."

Then the powerful-muscled missionary asked us what at first sounded like a foolish question. It was, "And I suppose you saved him by standing on safe ground yourself and telling him that, if he wanted to get home, all he would need to do would be to follow you in the path and he'd get there all right?"

"No sir," Little Jim said. "We got a homemade rope out to him and pulled him in."

"Oh, I see," John said. "You thought he

needed more than a good example. He needed to be saved *before* he could follow you home."

I knew he was trying to tell us something important, though I wasn't sure just what. But I happened just then to think of a Bible verse we'd had at our table one morning that says, "For the Son of Man has come to seek and to save that which was lost." My own father had said that morning, "No one can go to heaven by following Jesus as a good example. He needs to be saved first. Then he can follow Him."

For some reason my eyes began to sting a little, so I looked toward the Maple Leaf to see what Mrs. Fenwick was doing. She was looking up into the lower branches of the tree the cabin was named after, her eyes searching in as many different directions as there are. She brought her eyes back when Big Jim went on explaining the map.

"Right at this place marked with the red X is where you can leave the swamp and go on up to Old Man Paddler's cabin . . ."

It didn't take long to show the Fenwicks all the places of special interest in the area—though we had to watch that everything Big Jim pointed out didn't start Dragonfly on a stammering story of something exciting or dangerous that had happened there.

"As for the creek itself, you'll want to watch especially close to the island, where the water is shallow. There are hidden rocks that could damage your propeller. And up here just below the bridge is the big rock, with its wide flat surface, where the soft-shelled turtles take their afternoon naps.

"To the left of the rock," he went on "—you can see it as you look down from the bridge—is the deep pool where Old Whopper hangs out. That's the oldest and biggest bass in the creek. Every fisherman who comes here has tried to land him, but the old boy is too smart for them, and—"

Big Jim stopped and looked away from the map toward the big rock itself. "And if you don't mind our saying so, we hope he'll *always* be here. The creek wouldn't be the same if we couldn't stand on the bridge and toss a stone down into the water near his hiding place and see him go charging out after it like a dog chasing a stick, then stare at it and give a disgusted flip of his tail and sink back into his hideout again."

Elona Fenwick let out a little squeal right then and said, "Look! There's our first hummingbird!"

We all looked where she was looking, which was toward a hummingbird feeder, filled with what I supposed was red sweetened water. There was one of nature's finest sights, a ruby-throated hummingbird, its wings beating the air as fast and furious as the feathery wings of the giant sphinx moth that darts around our house at twilight and at night, sipping nectar out of the heart of Mom's petunias.

For a second, I liked Elona Fenwick even better because she liked birds.

Back again to the map, Big Jim had just started talking when Dragonfly cut in again to exclaim, "Look, everybody! There's old Long Neck Blue, down by the island!"

Big Jim frowned a little, but he joined the rest of us in looking toward the island below us, maybe two hundred yards away. And we all got a fine look at a great blue heron. It was the only one we'd ever seen in the territory, unless part of the time we saw him, he was not *him* but *her.* His very beautiful blue heron wife would look exactly like him.

Old Long Neck's upper parts are a slate-colored blue. His stomach, I remembered from having seen him up close once, is streaked with black and white. His long, sharp bill is part yellow, and the one long leg he was standing on right that minute in the shallow water at the island's edge was as black as coal soot.

We knew that when old Long Neck Blue was standing like that, he wasn't asleep, as it says in a certain poem about horses, which "hang their sleepy heads and stand still in a stall." But the heron's sharp eyes were watching for a fish or frog to get too close or for a dobsonfly to accidentally light in the water in front of him. Or maybe the larva of a dobsonfly would wriggle a little from under a rock.

Then like a streak of gray, blue, and yellow lightning, his long, sharp bill would shoot into the water, and the minnow or frog or the dobsonfly's larva would go on the "long, long trail a-winding" down old Long Neck's long neck into his first stomach. Then, a little later, nature would empty it into his second stomach, which is called the gizzard, where it would be ground into digestible size, and—well, that would be the end of the frog or minnow or anything else old Long Neck's long neck could swallow whole.

I don't know what happened right then. Maybe it was another one of Elona's squeals about the hummingbird. Anyway, all of a sudden, old Blue came to awkward life. He swooshed up into the air and took off, his long, angular wings taking him in the direction of the swamp and the mouth of the cave. Both long, thin legs were dangling, their claws spread like the roots of a giant ragweed a boy has just pulled out of a fencerow and shaken the dirt off of.

It seemed we had maybe stayed long enough at the Maple Leaf, and after saying and getting quite a few friendly good-byes, we left, going past the dock to the path that led to the bridge.

Back on the other side, we took off on the run to the spring for a drink, then hurried on to the swimming hole. We would have just time for a good swim before having to go home and report to our folks.

Big Jim stopped in the middle of taking off his T-shirt and asked, "Well, gang, what do you think of our new neighbors?"

Knowing no one could hear us except ourselves, I came out with, "Anybody who likes birds, might like boys. And anybody who likes boys, and understands them, is a human being. Did you see the way her eyes lit up when the hummingbird took his first drink of nectar from her feeder?"

Dragonfly, his own T-shirt already off and his bare white chest exposed to the breeze from the creek, sneezed. Then he surprised us by saying, "She's the prettiest missionary I ever saw." And then his dragonfly-like eyes looked away bashfully, as though what he had said was a secret in his own mind and he was sorry he had let anybody else know it.

Poetry had been chinning himself on a branch of the Snatzerpazooka tree on which we were hanging our clothes. He puffed out his thoughts, which were, "She bakes wonderful cookies."

"Cookies!" Little Jim squeaked. "My own mother baked those cookies!"

Big Jim broke into the conversation, reminding us, "Up to now, nobody has said anything about *Mr.* Fenwick," which up to now no one had.

Circus was the first to say what he thought. "I'm not sure how *smart* they are—to be taken in by a boy we all know is an ornery rascal."

"Shorty's smart," I put in. "He can be polite when he wants to."

Big Jim flexed his biceps, opened and closed his large fists a few times, admired the brown muscles below his elbows, and ventured,

"Did you see his arm and shoulder muscles—strong enough to bend an iron rod into a hoop."

Dragonfly was looking down at his own thin, white straight muscles when he thought to say, "He didn't look like anything was wrong with him. How come his doctor told him he had to take a vacation and not work for a long time?"

Just looking at Dragonfly's spindly arms was enough to make a boy sneeze, which he did right then, looking south toward the sun to help him get the sneeze out into the open. At the end of his long-tailed sneeze, he raised his voice to say, "Look! There's Old Granny Woody, frozen stiff!"

We all looked where Dragonfly was looking, across the narrow neck of red clover to a little brown knoll near the thicket that borders the bayou. Sure enough, there was Old Granny Woody, the biggest, grizzliest groundhog there ever was, maybe. She was one of our best animal brothers, though we could never get very close to her because she wouldn't let us.

There were maybe twenty groundhogs in the neighborhood. But they never seemed to do anybody any real harm, except that once in a while, when they were hungry, they would sneak into somebody's garden and eat a few beans and peas.

Nearly every February 2, which is Groundhog Day all over America, some of the gang would get up before sunrise and sneak down along the bayou, hide behind the thicket, and watch to see if Granny would come out of her burrow to see her shadow. Groundhogs, like bears, are hibernators. They sleep all winter and wake up and come out only after a long winter's nap.

Granny had lived in her network of tunnels by the bayou for as far back as I can remember. She was as much a part of the territory as the squirrels and rabbits or mayapples or wild rosebushes or even as Old Whopper, Chippy-chip-chee, and Long Neck Blue. She was just like one of the family.

What Dragonfly meant when he said Old Granny was "frozen stiff" was that she had reared up on her haunches and was standing as straight and stiff as the stump of a willow or elm sapling after a beaver has cut down its tree. Like a gopher or chipmunk, when Granny gets scared or suspicious of something or somebody, she will do that and will stay "frozen" until she is sure it is safe to move. Or if she is *really* scared, she will drop to the ground and scramble like a grizzly brown streak of scared lightning for her den or to some other place of safety.

Granny, standing now like a statue, thinking and maybe wondering what on earth, would never get killed or hurt by any of us. Her one short ear, nipped off once when she got caught in somebody's sharp-jawed trap, would always let us know who she was, if we happened to see her playing with a lot of other woodchucks anywhere.

"Good Old Granny Woody!" Little Jim said. "She's my very best woodchuck friend."

And then, *then,* and *double then!* That is when we heard the sharp crack of a rifle and saw a puff of blue smoke rise from behind the thicket. At that same instant, Granny Woody leaped up into the air and spun around. Then she dropped to the grassy knoll she had been frozen on and began to twist and writhe and go into a tangled-up spasm like a cat having a fit, crashing all around, clawing the air, and twitching.

At almost the same time, a boy's high-pitched excited voice yelled from the thicket, "I've got 'im! I've killed a groundhog!"

Hearing that piercing, screaming voice, which I'd heard too many times in my half-long life, and knowing whose bragging voice it was, I felt my teeth clamp shut and my temple muscles harden. "Shorty Long!" I exclaimed. "He's killed Granny!"

Like a big, two-legged, giant-sized woodchuck, my worst enemy dashed out from behind the bushes and streaked toward the knoll, where Granny was giving the last few sad twitches of her dying body. He grabbed her up by the tail and, with his rifle in one hand and the limp groundhog in the other, came dragging her toward us.

4

I stood as stock-still as a frozen woodchuck, wondering what on earth and why.

It took only a few seconds for Shorty Long to drag Granny to where we were. Quicker than a referee blowing a whistle when he sees a foul in a basketball game, he stood his .22 against the trunk of the Snatzerpazooka tree. Then, before any of us could have stopped him, even if we had known what he was going to do, he grabbed Granny Woody's tail with both hands. He half dragged and half carried her to the creek, spun around twice in a wide circle like a discus thrower in a track meet, and hurled that heavy, short-tailed "terrestrial squirrel"—which is what the dictionary says a woodchuck really is—up and out and out and out and out, where she landed with a noisy splash right in the middle of our swimming hole.

The waves from the splash spread into a widening circle, leaving Granny floating in the middle like flotsam from a shipwreck. Her own happy life was the ship. Her dead body was all that was left of it.

"There, you thief!" Shorty Long shouted in the direction of Granny Woody's gray-haired body. "That'll teach you to keep your ornery little family out of our garden, eating up my mother's peas and beans and lettuce!"

With that, Shorty Long strutted back toward us, reached for his rifle, and started down the path that goes toward the spring. There was a smirk on his face that said, "I think a lot of myself! I'm a very important person!"

"Stop!" Big Jim's voice barked.

And Shorty Long did. He swung around with his rifle raised—though not pointing toward any of us, because no person who knows how to handle guns would ever let his gun be pointed on purpose or even accidentally toward anything or anybody he doesn't intend to shoot.

"Did you say," Big Jim's voice asked accusingly, "that you *knew* Granny had a family of groundhog babies?"

"Certainly!" Shorty called back in short, sharp words. "Four of 'em! I've got four traps set at the place where she always led them through the fence. She taught them to be thieves!"

Little Jim, who hardly ever gets his temper up, came to fiery life with his voice right then, yelling, "They're not thieves! They don't know it's wrong! They're just *hungry*, that's all!"

Shorty shrugged his shoulders, smirked a sideways smirk, and barked back to us, "Your old Granny is not the only varmint that's going to get shot this summer. The pigeons that keep nesting in our barn and scatter their droppings all over our alfalfa hay, the rats that steal corn out of our corncrib, the squirrels that steal our walnuts, the coons that steal our eggs and chickens, the weasels and owls and—"

"Owls," I cut in on him to disagree, "are a farmer's best friend. They eat cutworms, mice, and—"

"Also, little old Daisy Lee here"—Shorty cut *me* short, lifting his rifle and patting its walnut-colored stock—"is going to protect me in case one of your bigger 'brothers' gets too friendly, such as a wildcat or a bear. Remember, you killed a bear once yourselves. So you needn't be so uppity about a boy protecting himself!"

And with that, Shorty Long took a parting shot at us. "I'll have to hurry on down to the Maple Leaf. Uncle John's expecting me. He's going to teach me to run the outboard this morning, and I'm going to show him and Aunt Elona all around—all the good fishing places and where the dangerous underwater rocks are. We might even catch Old Whopper. Who knows?"

Big Jim called after him again, "What do you mean—'Uncle John'?"

Shorty Long answered in a scornful voice, "Didn't you know? Uncle John and Aunt Elona have adopted me. I'm going to be their nephew while they're here!"

And then, in a teacher tone, he called back to us, "Class is dismissed!" He turned and, carrying his rifle as if he was looking for anything that moved so that he could shoot it, he swung into the path that leads to the spring and the leaning linden tree, on his way to take a ride in the *Vida Eterna.*

I stood with set jaw and tense temple muscles, watching the movement of the tall weeds that bordered the path Shorty Long was working his way along. All of us were still standing frozen, our eyes and minds on fire with anger and with what my mother sometimes calls "frustration." That was *her* "word for the day" one day last week. It's the feeling a dog gets when it is trailing a fox or coon and accidentally loses the scent and goes running all over everywhere trying to find it and can't and finally has to give up.

There wasn't a thing we could do about Shorty Long. Not one single thing. Now that he had a new rifle, he felt very brave and a very important person, and he had his mind made up to keep on being the kind of a boy he was. What could you do with a boy like that?

I didn't know I was humming a tune in my mind, or that the words were going to ooze out and be heard by anybody, until Little Jim, who was closest to me at the time, said, "My mother listens to that program every morning. It helps her have a good day."

"What program?" I asked. Then I heard the words that were tumbling over each other in my mind. They were "Every day's a wonderful day," which *this* day wasn't!

It wasn't even a wonderful *minute,* because from the direction of the linden tree right that *very* minute there was another rifle shot. And with my mind's eye I saw a red squirrel or maybe a flying squirrel or a cottontail lying dead on the ground.

"I'll bet he's shot Chippy-chip-chee!" Circus cried.

And I figured that was exactly what Shorty had done. He'd spotted the cute little chipmunk, which always used the Black Widow Stump for his lookout, taken a bead on him with his new .22, and killed him.

"Come on!" Big Jim ordered us. "Let's go see." He broke into a gallop with five barefoot boys lighting out after him as fast as we could go.

Poetry, puffing along behind me, asked in a frustrated voice, "What if he decides old Long Neck Blue is a varmint!"

"Varmints," as most any farm or ranch boy knows, is the name hunters give to small animals that make themselves a nuisance around the neighborhood, such as rats, mice, and weasels.

As we panted along, I said to Poetry over my shoulder, "Shorty Long is the *biggest* varmint in the whole country!"

Before we reached the board fence that separated the nettle patch from the spring, we heard another shot, and, as we came storming up the incline to the base of the leaning linden tree, there was still another crack from Shorty's rifle.

We burst out into the open, expecting to see Chippy-chip-chee lying dead or dying at the base of the Black Widow Stump, and maybe the big Long boy standing gloating over him. But instead, I saw Shorty over in the direction of the bridge, his rifle lifted and pointed toward a large nest of leaves high in the top of the butternut tree that grew there.

Again there was the sharp, ear-jarring crack of a rifle and a puff of gray blue smoke. And from that leafy nest there was a rustling movement followed by a flurry of rusty brown wildlife.

One of the more than twenty flying squirrels we knew lived in the woods came streaking out of the nest. He crawled in a hurry to the end of a long branch and poised a second. Then, like a boy taking a headfirst leap from a high diving board into a swimming pool, that cute little animal brother of ours spread its flying membrane and took off for the ground. He glided in a long slant in the direction of the base of another butternut tree, where he landed in a grassy place with a *plop-plop*. In a streak of a second he was on his way up that tree, climbing as fast as a cat scared of a dog, up and up and round and round to the very top, and out to the end of a long branch. There he spread his sails again, and away he went.

It was a fine sight—that cute little, smart little, scared little not-varmint was up maybe five trees and down again in only a few excited minutes. He got almost as far as the papaw bushes before he disappeared into a den in the top of the old maple growing there.

All this time, the boy with the rifle acted as if he didn't know we were watching him. He kept his eyes focused on the fleeing flying squirrel. Then he shrugged like the fox in a certain fable every boy knows, who seemed to say, "Those old grapes are sour. They're not fit for a fine fox like me!"

Shorty looked at his wristwatch and took off down the path to the bridge, where, after he crossed it, he could go down the embankment to the Maple Leaf and the new white boat—and where he could begin to be the very polite, courteous, adopted nephew of a missionary. It seemed he was a kind of boy angel when he was with the Fenwicks and a *not*-angel when he was with us.

It also seemed not a one of us could say a word. There was a mixed-up feeling in my mind that I couldn't handle and didn't understand until Circus broke our tense silence by saying, "He didn't even look at us! What's he think we are anyway? Some kind of doormats to wipe his feet on?"

That, Bill Collins, I thought, *explains the way you feel. A boy can't stand being ignored, even by his enemy.*

Then from behind me, interrupting the stormy weather in my mind, there came the friendly, coaxing voice of Little Jim, saying, "Come on, Chippy. Come on! We won't hurt you! Here's a little snack I brought for you."

Swinging my eyes toward the Black Widow Stump, I saw the curly-haired, cutest member of the gang down on his haunches, holding out his hand. And coming timidly toward him was

Chippy-chip-chee, bouncing his tail and making quick little runs and starts and stops toward an unshelled peanut that Little Jim had just tossed out to him.

It was like coming out of a tornado, safe and sound, into a very friendly sunshiny day.

Taking a final look toward the bridge, I saw, way out in the middle on his way across, a boy in tan slacks, carrying a rifle and sort of strutting along as if he was the king of the world and the boss of all the people in it.

Chippy-chip-chee made a quick short run, grabbed up little Jim's peanut, and, like a streak of happiness, took off for the stump. He scooted up its bark-covered side, perched himself on his haunches, held the peanut in his front paws, and chewed away on it.

For a few minutes it seemed a very peaceful world. But we hadn't any sooner started up the long wildflower-bordered barefoot boys' footpath toward our house, where we would separate and each go his own way to report to his parents what nice human beings the Fenwicks were, than there came the crack of a rifle from somewhere down the creek.

We all stopped and stared at each other's startled face, not a one of us saying anything until Big Jim came out with, "Maybe he thinks soft-shelled turtles are targets." He clenched his teeth, and his eyes were squinting from thinking hard thoughts.

Little Jim spoke next, and his trembling voice showed that the fire in Big Jim's tone had set fire to his mind. "A bullet could kill Old Whopper too! If it happened to hit the rock and glance off into the water!"

Well, we had to go on. Pretty soon it would be lunchtime. And no matter how good an excuse we might think we had for being late, it wouldn't be worth all the words we would have to use to explain it to our folks.

We had work to do all afternoon. Little Jim had his piano lesson to take. Poetry had to help his father build a new hog house. Big Jim and Circus, living close to each other, were going to work in each other's gardens. Dragonfly was supposed to help his mother around the Tall Corn Motel, this being the beginning of the tourist season for them. And I, Bill Collins—sometimes called William Jasper Collins when my father, Theodore, thought I had done something wrong and needed to be talked to and at—had to work in our own garden with the Ebenezer onions, the Alderman peas, the pole beans, and the Early Egyptian beets.

When I came into the yard, Mom was on the phone with somebody—some other Sugar Creek mother, maybe—and I got to the yellow rosebush just outside the window in time to hear her say in her most cheerful telephone voice, "I think that's just wonderful, Mrs. Long. Just wonderful. You can put that down as an answer to prayer."

Then, seeing me standing outside, she said into the phone, "Here's Bill now. He'll be glad to hear it, I'm sure."

But I wasn't glad to hear it. What Mom told me then just couldn't be the truth. It just *couldn't* be!

Can you imagine what my wonderful gray-brown-haired mother told me Shorty Long's mother could put down as an answer to prayer? This is what:

"For a week now, ever since the Fenwicks arrived in the States, Shorty has been behaving like a little gentleman, being especially courteous around the home, doing helpful things without having to be reminded several times—things like that.

"And because today is his birthday, his father gave him the new rifle he'd been wanting and had been promised, if he earned it with good behavior."

I just couldn't tell Mom what had come into my mind right then. My mother was the teacher of the women's Sunday school class at our church. All the women in the class called her about their home problems as well as asking Bible questions, and Mom got an answer to some prayer or other almost every day for some of the mothers. How could I tell her that Shorty Guenther Long was *not* a better boy—was maybe even worse—and that he had only been pretending to be good just to get the rifle no boy with *his* mind should ever have!

"I'll wash up and help set the table," I offered and started toward the iron pitcher pump, near which we kept our outdoor washstand, a hand towel, and soap.

Right that minute my little sister, Charlotte Ann, was trying to pump the pump to get a drink she maybe didn't need. She was always pumping herself about thirty drinks a day.

This time, though, she wasn't getting a drink for herself but for her favorite doll, Elsie Jo. "Elsie Jo's terribly thirsty," my shining-eyed, dark-haired, rosy-cheeked, extrapretty three-year-old sister looked up at me and said.

I helped her fill Elsie's bottle and warned her, "You have to be careful with Elsie Jo when you're around the water trough. She hasn't learned to swim yet, and she might drown. Promise me you'll be careful."

Charlotte Ann was already on her way to the doll buggy by the side porch and didn't hear me—or wasn't interested, anyway, but only wanted to help Elsie Jo drink her water.

I got the washbasin from its stand near the grape arbor and carried it to the pump platform, gave the pump a few fast, squeaking strokes, carried the water back to the stand, and reached for the bar of soap we keep there. I was scrubbing away when I noticed Mixy, our old black-and-white cat, taking a dust bath beside the hollyhocks. She was rolling over and over the way cats do, getting her ordinarily shining fur a rusty brown color.

A second later, Mixy was finished with her bath. Maybe deciding she needed a little love, she began to stroke herself by brushing back and forth against and between my ankles.

At almost the same minute, Charlotte Ann

decided she had been without a brother long enough or else Elsie Jo had stopped crying for a drink. Anyway, my very pretty, dark-haired, long-eyelashed, brown-eyed sister came toddling over to wash *her* hands in my sudsy water.

Well, seeing those little brown, suntanned hands rinsing themselves in water that was a lot more soiled than *they* were gave me a very proud feeling toward the only sister I had up to now. It was as cheerful a feeling as I get sometimes when I see a saucy little whirlwind spiraling out across the south pasture. I quickly stop whatever I am doing and go chasing after it, toss myself into it, and dodge my way along in it until all of a sudden it whirls itself into nothing.

Quicker than a meadowlark's melody that seems to come from all around you, and you don't know where it is and can't see it, my glad feeling made me quickly dry my hands on the roller towel that hung from the grape arbor crossbeam, swoop my sister up into my arms, and start stumbling along with her toward the house, where in a few minutes lunch would be ready. Charlotte Ann was squealing and giggling all the way, as though she liked her big brother even better than she did Elsie Jo.

I managed to open the screen door and squeeze through. Charlotte Ann was still happy and laughing. But Mixy squeezed through behind me and sailed, with bushy tail upright, straight through the kitchen into the living room, just in time for Mom to see her and call out, “Don’t let that cat in! You know what she does when she gets in!”

I set my sister down with a swoosh, dived into the living room after Mixy, and got there just in time to see her make a Jack-be-nimble, Jack-be-quick jump onto Mom’s neatly made bed in the bedroom that is just off the living room. She landed right in the middle of Mom’s brand-new, green-and-white-striped, extrafancy bedspread! And on top of that—on top of the bedspread, I mean—our black-and-white and dusty brown cat rolled happily over and over and over!

5

But a mother's green-and-white brand-new bedspread is no place for a black-and-white and dusty brown cat to wallow in like a bear wallowing in a swamp or Old Red Addie in her favorite wallowing place behind the barn.

In less time than it would take for a rooster to crow in the morning, I scooped up Mixy, carried her to the front door, and dashed out into the yard. I tossed her overboard, dropping her upside down in a grassy place behind the yellow rosebush, and saying to her with a scolding voice, "Flotsam, jetsam, and lagan! You can decide for yourself which of the three you want to be!"

But that cat landed on her feet, and, before I could turn to go back into the house, she spied a milkweed butterfly loping along in the air near the peony bush. She took off after it as if she was as innocent as the blood red peony flowers themselves.

When I came back into the house again, Mom was standing just inside the bedroom door, staring down at her new bedspread as though she couldn't believe it. There were tears in her eyes, and I knew there was a storm in her heart.

Trying to think of something cheerful to

say at a time like that, I could think of only one word, and it was, "Frustrations?"

Still standing and looking, Mom nodded, while Charlotte Ann, whose happiness had been to blame for starting everything, tugged at Mom's apron, saying with a whining voice, "I'm hungry!"

And *that* reminded Mom of something in the kitchen. The smell and smoke of something hot and maybe burning on the stove also reminded her. She came back into her mother's world as fast as the man in the poem "The Night Before Christmas," when out on the lawn he heard such a clatter, he sprang from his bed to see what was the matter.

I got to the kitchen myself in time to see her quickly pick up a potholder, grab a skillet of something burning on the range, and dive to the back door with it to keep the smoke from smoking up the whole house. The kitchen was already so thick with it you could hardly see.

"I'll get the table set," I offered again, and Mom didn't say a word. Her lips were pressed tightly together. There was a Shorty Long in her life, too, I happened to think. And for some reason I had a feeling that was as kind and wonderful as the one I had had when a few minutes before I'd looked down into the shining eyes of my sister, Charlotte Ann.

I tried to think of something to say to Mom that would be as good as a pain pill for a headache, but I could only manage to come up with, "Don't you care too much, Mom. Remember, I'm on your team, and we're in the same game together. I made a bad fumble without intending to, and the bedspread's my fault. If you have to send it to the cleaners, I'll pay for it out of my allowance."

I had washed my hands of Mixy's dusty fur and was laying the knives and forks in their places on each side of the plates when, from behind me, Mom put her left cheek against my right one and said, "I'm on your side, too, and we both have Someone else fighting for us."

Then she added, as she turned on the fan to blow the smoke out of the kitchen, "What's a little old bedspread anyway! Maybe I was too proud of it. Too proud, too, of the way I had the eggs fried exactly right!"

That's when I remembered something I'd heard Dad say once, which was, "There are two kinds of 'proud'—the kind that is right and another kind that is selfish. A man *has* to have pride in his work and do it the best he can. But if his pride is selfish and snobbish, it's the kind the Bible condemns when it says, 'Pride goes before destruction, and a haughty spirit before stumbling.'"

It seemed a good time to quote Dad's words the best I could remember them. I started to, but Mom interrupted me, maybe without knowing she was doing it, by saying, "It's an answer to prayer."

Astonished, I asked, *"What is?"* I wondered how burned food, a smoke-filled kitchen, and a soiled new bedspread *could* be.

I got a nice surprise when Mom answered as if she were talking to somebody else in the room. "The peace You have just given me."

I was whistling a tune of some kind in my mind as she took three eggs from the basket in the corner and started over again to fry them exactly right. Then my whispered whistle turned into an out loud one, and the song was "Every Day's a Wonderful Day!"

It kept on being a wonderful day in spite of a lot of little upsets and almost too much flotsam, jetsam, and lagan, as Mom and Charlotte Ann and I lived our way through it with the help of an innocent, never guilty green-eyed cat.

I swung into the after-lunch work, stopping now and then to feel my muscles to see if they were strong as iron bands. Some of them seemed they were. It felt good to know that when Dad would get home from Indianapolis late that night, all the chores would be done. And I would be proud in the right way that I had done them myself, even if I might not ever be given a new rifle for my birthday.

It was five o'clock in the afternoon and time to gather the eggs when from the house Mom's voice quavered out across the barnyard to where I was, near Addie's apartment. "Bill! Yoo-hoo! Telephone! Poetry!"

I swung out of Addie's sty, dashed through the gate, shut it with a bang, and raced to the house, stopping only long enough to give my feet several fast swishes on the doormat. Then I went quickly through the kitchen into the living room and answered the phone by the east window.

"Just thought you'd like to know," Poetry said in a low, secretive kind of voice, "that a white boat with a boy in it is racing up and down the creek, cutting wide circles, stirring up heavy waves, and sending them crashing against the shore, and maybe scaring the daylights out of all the fish in the creek."

And now, I ask you, what can a boy or a gang of boys do about a thing like that? What *can* he or they do?

The house of my mind was filled with the smoke of something burning when I finished talking and listening to Poetry. Mom was upstairs at the time, looking after something or other, so I went out through the kitchen to the back door, stomped past the iron pitcher pump, and on to the garden gate.

The Ebenezer onions, the Alderman peas, the pole beans, the Scarlet Globe and White Icicle radishes needed weeding and cultivating, all right, and I didn't mind using my muscles on them. *But how,* I asked myself, *can you get the noxious jimsonweeds out of the mind of a boy like Shorty Long? How can you?*

Spying a little patch of six-inch-tall pigweeds at the edge of the garden, I grabbed up a handful, gave them a yank, and threw them as hard as I could toward Old Red Addie, where they landed right in front of her snuffling snout. She took a lazy sniff at them, looked up, and walked over to her long wooden trough as much as to say, "I'm hungry! How long before supper is ready?" Then she started squealing and grunting as though she was the most neglected hog in the country.

"Look," I said down to her, "you don't know what trouble is!"

Leaving Addie to her worries, I went back to my own. One thought was milling around in my mind. It was something my father had once said to me. "If you want to wash the temper out of your mind, hard work is the best soap there is."

In a few minutes I was scrubbing away on my angry mind by chasing around from one hen's nest to another. I looked in the toolshed, in seven or eight coops along the orchard fence, and up in the haymow, where my favorite laying hen, old Bent Comb, sometimes laid her daily egg in a nest under a log. *Where,* I asked myself, *is that rascal of a hen laying her eggs now?* It had been more than a week since she'd laid any eggs in the nest I was looking at right that minute.

Come to think of it, I thought, *where is she herself?* I hadn't seen her all day. Or for several days.

Maybe I ought to tell you that, beside hard work, I had found another way to get my temper under control. It was even better than Dad's method. My mind was still smoking a little when I climbed up over the alfalfa to a secret place in the far corner of the haymow.

There I reached into a crack in a log, took out a smallish brown leather book, and opened it. It was kind of like looking in the dictionary for a word for the day. My word for the *minute* right then was: "Your word I have treasured in my heart, that I may not sin against You."

I wasn't quite sure how to treasure God's Word in my heart, but it seemed that maybe if I would memorize the verse and keep saying it over and over again to myself, it would be the same as treasuring it. My short prayer to the One who made boys and the whole wide world, and even the universes out in space, didn't sound very much like our pastor's prayer, but part of it was: "Maybe You could help the gang do something about Shorty Long, so we won't make him any worse than he is. If You made him the same as You did us, how come he is so ornery?"

I didn't hear any answer from God, but all of a sudden I thought a thought I'd never thought before, and it was: *Shorty Long is trying to do his own making, and he is doing a bad job of it. Anybody who wants to be a better boy will have to turn his life over to Somebody who knows how to make him better.*

As soon as my eyes were open again, I looked out through a crack between the weatherboarding and saw, away up near the twin pignut trees at the farther end of the garden, my smallish sister, all alone, toddling around in the clover. She was running back and forth and stopping now and then to look all around and up into the trees. Listening to see if I could hear her fussing about anything, which she sometimes does about almost nothing, I heard her singing a song we sometimes sing in the primary department at Sunday school, and it was

"This little light of mine,
I'm going to let it shine;
This little light of mine,
I'm going to let it shine, let it shine,
Let it shine, let it shine."

I couldn't hear all the words, but I knew what they were from having heard and sung them myself when I was little.

Pretty soon I was down the haymow ladder and looking for more eggs. As soon as I was outdoors, Charlotte Ann spotted me and began to call me to come and help her find her red ball.

With her little light trying to shine in my mind, I took my time moseying up to her, looking all along the fencerow of the garden to see if I could find old Bent Comb's nest. And that's when I *did* find it. It was beyond the pignut trees and under the weed-grown lower rail of the garden fence, with Charlotte Ann's red ball right beside it. And on the nest was Bent Comb herself.

"Hey, young lady!" I said down to her. "What are you doing still on your nest this late in the afternoon? You're the only hen in the flock who's not already laid her egg for the day!"

She cocked her saucy head at me, her fiery red bent comb almost hiding her left eye. She squatted a little lower and wider and stayed where she was.

"Look!" I ordered her. "You can't stay in bed all day and all night too. Up! Out!" I reached for her to pick her up by the feathers on her back. And what on my wondering right hand did I get but several short, sharp, savage pecks!

Charlotte Ann was tugging at me now, begging me to come and play ball with her, but I wouldn't. I couldn't until I found out what my curiosity told me to find out about old Bent Comb.

Very carefully, so as not to be a henpecked boy, I managed to ease that snow-white leghorn off her nest. Then I saw in a quick count that she had maybe seven eggs, as many as she could have laid at the rate of one a day for a week—which was as long as Mom had been missing her.

While I was quickly counting and thinking, Bent Comb was cluck-clucking like a fussing old setting hen, as if she were trying to say, "For goodness' sake! Let me alone! I'm going to raise a family!" She then came to angry hen life again and let loose with several more short, sharp, savage pecks.

"OK! OK!" I answered, lifting the back of my hand to my lips.

"What's the matter with her?" Charlotte Ann wanted to know as she both helped and hindered me in carrying the egg basket toward the house.

My answer was something like this: "Old Bent Comb's lonesome. She wants a family of baby chickens, and the only way to get them is to sit for three weeks on a nest of eggs. When the three weeks are over and the fluffy little babies are out and cheeping and running all over the place following her around, she'll be happy again."

I didn't get to finish my lesson in nature, because the only pupil in my one-pupil barnyard school was already halfway to the grape arbor, chasing after a red ball she had thrown on ahead of her.

I looked down at my henpecked hand, and one of the peck marks was bleeding a little. Then I said in a teacher voice to myself, "Maybe you're learning something, Bill Collins! The wood thrush doesn't like it when her nest is disturbed; Old Bent Comb gets mad when you disturb her nest; and the Sugar Creek Gang gets upset when anything upsets the peace and quiet of *their* nest."

Our nest was the whole Sugar Creek territory, which we'd had for our playground all our lives. It seemed we had a right to it without any cowbird or woodpecker or turkey buzzard—and it seemed Shorty Long was all three—trying to build another nest right beside ours!

All of a sudden there was a commotion in

the barnyard. Every hen and rooster everywhere began to cackle and run for the chicken house. Several of the old hens let out wild and excited squawks, while at the same time a dozen fluffy little chickens that had been following along after Rhodie Reddie, their Rhode Island Red mother, came racing toward her as though they were half scared to death.

I quick looked up toward to the sky to see how come they were so scared, and I saw a giant chicken hawk about to light in one of the pignut trees.

Two words—and they weren't words for the day, either—came rushing into my mind. They were "varmint" and "chicken hawk!" And Shorty Long was both of them too.

And then I thought something I maybe shouldn't have thought, because it didn't seem right to be thinking it. It was, *If the Fenwicks hadn't come, they wouldn't have brought the shining new boat Shorty acts like he owns. And if there hadn't been any missionary cabin so close to our playground—and even right in it—and if Old Man Paddler hadn't given the land to the church—and if—*

I had reached the back door with the egg basket by the time I'd thought all those half-ornery thoughts, getting there just in time to hear Mom humming the tune of a song we sometimes hear on a Western program. It was "Home on the Range"—which she was home on right that minute. The *stove* range, I mean.

"That you, Bill?" she asked cheerfully.

"Hurry and get washed up for supper. It'll be ready in a jiffy!"

It was maybe about nine o'clock at night before our car came through the front gate, stopped at the walnut tree, and Dad came hurrying across the moonlit yard to where Mom was waiting for him on the board walk not far from the pitcher pump and the grape arbor.

From where I was at the time, looking out the window of my upstairs room, it seemed maybe they hadn't been so glad to see each other for a long time. Mom kind of half ran from the pump platform to meet him in the middle of the yard under the spreading plum tree, and I heard her ask, "What kind of a day did you have?"

"Wonderful," Dad said. And after giving her a hug or two and they were on their way back to the house, he asked, "What kind of a day did *you* have?"

I couldn't hear all of Mom's answer because of the squeaking of the screen door when Dad opened it, but part of it was, "A dozen shipwrecks and lots of flotsam. I was a wreck myself several times. But Good Ship Bill was standing by to come to the rescue." It was something like that, anyway, which it didn't hurt me to hear.

They came into the house, and I stayed on at the window, looking out, listening to the plick-plocking of the crickets near the grape arbor and, from the woods, one of my favorite summer night sounds. An orchestra of maybe a hundred green, long-horned insects called katydids was rasping out, *"Katy did, Katy she did, Katy did, Katy she did . . ."* On and on and still on, their monotone melody made me sleepy just to hear them.

Yawning and already half asleep, I turned toward the turned-down bed, almost stumbling over the dictionary table. In the moonlight I could see that the biggest book in the house was still open, maybe to the very page it had been open to that morning. Dropping with a sigh onto the pillow, I heard my own monotone voice mumbling, "I wonder if there will be any flotsam floating around anywhere tomorrow. Or any jetsam or lagan."

Then, as it says in a poem somebody or other wrote, "No boy knows when he goes to sleep," I sailed off into the Land of Nod. And the next thing I knew, it was morning.

6

Even though old Bent Comb had helped me understand the gang's feelings about having our privacy invaded, for quite a while we still felt cranky as a wood thrush when a boy peeks into her nest. Every time we were in swimming with all our clothes off, which is the way we had done it all our half-long lives, we had to stop, look, and listen to see if anybody and his wife were out in an aluminum boat taking a ride in our direction.

They did surprise us once. The boat came from upstream instead of down, where we had thought they were, and we had to make a helter-skelter, topsy-turvy, splashy race for shore, grab our clothes from the Snatzerpazooka tree, and scatter into the tall corn.

After a while we began to get used to having company every day, though, and the Maple Leaf became a favorite meeting place, especially since we got invited to come at least one night a week for a wiener roast or a fish fry.

The very first week, John taught us something he had learned as a boy—how to do what is called trotline fishing. This is a very special kind of fishing, and some states have laws to control it. He called it Elona's trotline, and she was very proud of it. She was like a little girl who had been given a brand-new doll for her birthday or for Christmas.

Trotline fishing, in case you might like to know how to do it, is something like this: You stretch an extrastrong fishing line across the creek or partway across, with hooks suspended on fifteen-inch pieces of strong cord. You use a swivel halfway up each short, strong cord to keep it from twisting if you catch a fish on it.

Poetry brought a brick with holes in it to fasten to one end of the line. We sank it more than halfway across the creek. The other end of the long line we tied on the same shore as the Maple Leaf—to a smallish tree halfway between the dock and Old Whopper's rock-sheltered water house.

Before rowing the tied-on brick to the end of the line and sinking it, we had baited each of the fifteen hooks we were going to use with blobs of fishing worms. We had five other smaller sinkers spaced along the line so it would stay on the bottom, where anybody knows catfish like to feed and also where we knew there was a mud bottom, which made as good a place for catfish to live and play and have their being in as a mud wallow is good for Old Red Addie and her pigs.

Almost every night Elona would catch three or four catfish. The gang had a lot of fun watching her pull in the line—we helped her bait her hooks again—and also *not* so much fun helping her clean those slimy, beady-eyed, horned, fierce-looking, good-eating fish, which is why we had to have a fish fry more often than we did a wiener roast.

John, being a doctor, taught us how to give first aid for such things as snakebites, poison ivy, foreign bodies in the eye, drowning, and nosebleed. He told us what to do for anybody, such as a small child, who has eaten too many aspirins, thinking it was candy.

"Because you boys spend a lot of time along and in the creek, you ought to be very sure you know how to give first aid to a person who has drowned," he told us. Then he explained the different methods lifesavers use to revive a drowned person, saying seriously, "If you ever have to choose between the manual method and mouth-to-mouth, the very best way is mouth-to-mouth."

To be sure we all understood how to revive a drowned person, he had us take a written examination like the kind we take in school. And all the gang passed the test with good grades.

Another very important examination was on first aid for snakebite. It felt fine to know how to keep your head and save any boy's life if he accidentally got bitten by a rattler or if, when going through the swamp, he got fanged by a cottonmouth, which is a nickname for the water moccasin.

One thing we couldn't understand, as the summer flew along too fast, was how come the Fenwicks kept on liking Shorty Long so well and how come he was the only boy in the neighborhood who got to run the *Vida Eterna* all by himself, even though Shorty seemed to be a careful driver. Every few days he and John would go fishing alone far up the creek above the Long's ranch. And sometimes when they all of a sudden came putt-putting along where we were in swimming or close to where we were fishing, Shorty would be sitting in the stern of the boat, driving and guiding it, steering it carefully around the shoals, and always making a wide circle to the big rock where Old Whopper was still safe and sound.

Another thing that bothered me was that Shorty had stopped shooting "varmints," and he even came to Sunday school and church.

Poetry was pretty upset about Shorty's beginning to behave himself so well, and he told me so one Sunday between Sunday school and the morning worship service. We were outdoors at the time getting a drink from the long-handled iron pump across the road from the church, waiting for the bell to ring. He handed me a cup of water as he said, "I don't get it! How come all of a sudden Shorty Long is an angel? Or how come he is an angel with John and Elona and a not-angel when he is with us?"

"The trouble is," I answered him, "all our mothers think he is getting to be so polite—even more polite than their own children!"

Saying that, I looked across the elm-shaded lane to the church entrance, where right that very minute our not-angel friend was going up the steps. I felt my eyes squinting, my jaw and temple muscles tensing.

Poetry must have been feeling the same as I, except that he was keeping his mind under better control. His eyes were on Shorty Long, too, at first. Then he finished his drink and looked around for a place to toss the leftover water in his cup. Spying a wild carrot growing in the fencerow behind the pump platform, he moved toward it and poured the water into its half-opened flower, which when it is only half opened is like a lace-bordered bird's nest. That is why the wild carrot around Sugar Creek is sometimes called a bird's nest. It is the most hated weed on the Collins farm because, if you give it a chance, in a few years it will take over a whole field.

"Here," Poetry said to the wild carrot, "is a little drink for you. You are the most hated weed in the county, so your short life will not be long."

With that, Poetry stooped, broke off the weak stem of the Queen Anne's lace, which is another name farmers use for the wild carrot, and, swinging his right arm in a wide circle, threw the whole plant as hard as he could in the direction of the front door of the Sugar Plain Schoolhouse, finishing with, "Class is dismissed!"

The church bell rang then, and we started on the run for the front door. Then we walked like boy angels up the same steps Wild Carrot Long had climbed three minutes earlier.

Inside and seated in the quiet church, I looked way down to the right of the pulpit to where, seated at the organ, was Little Jim's mother, playing "Break Thou the Bread of Life," her fingers walking carefully around over the keys. The music made a boy want to be quiet and behave himself a little better after he got home.

Knowing the whole song by heart from having sung it so many times, my mind took me on a sightseeing trip away back into the history section of Palestine. And I saw the Savior taking up five loaves of bread, breaking them into small pieces, and handing the pieces to the disciples, who carried the broken bread to the hundreds of people scattered all over the mountainside. It seemed that maybe, if I were the kind of disciple I ought to be, I would help pass the bread to somebody who was hungry.

Poetry, sitting beside me, eased his elbow into my side, and I came back from Galilee in time to start singing with the others.

That afternoon the gang stopped at the Maple Leaf to see if there was anything we could do for the Fenwicks. While we drank another cup apiece of Costa Rican punch, Elona told us something that helped us understand a little better what was going on in Shorty Long's mind. Shorty and John were out in the boat right that very minute, far up the creek.

"John and I used to have a boy just Shorty's age, and he looked very much like him. Well, the Lord allowed our son to die and go on ahead of us to heaven. It has been especially hard for John all these years. Now that he won't be able to be a missionary again for a long time —maybe never—he's even more lonely. You understand, don't you?"

I was looking up at the hummingbird feeder at the time, watching a ruby-throated hummer poised in the air, his wings holding him as safe as if he were on a twig. Then like a flash of feathery lightning, he pushed his long, sharp proboscis into the feeder tube, took a short sweet sip, and flashed away, skimming straight for the dock post at the end of the pier, where he perched as if he was short of breath and needed a rest.

I wasn't sure I understood—not Shorty, anyway—but I think I did understand big John Fenwick better.

In that fast second, I felt myself liking Shorty's Uncle John very, very, very much, and I didn't exactly hate Shorty Long. I even almost halfway liked him.

There wasn't anything in particular we could do at the Maple Leaf then, so we moseyed down to the empty dock, filed past and along the shore to the bridge, crossed it, and took the side path to the papaw bushes. Already the papaw fruit was beginning to ripen, I noticed. It had turned a brownish color like ripe bananas. I knew that on the inside of each papaw was a yellowish custard center with flat brown seeds as big as marbles. The papaw leaves themselves were maybe twelve inches long and hung in clusters all over the bushes like long, wide, flat green icicles.

There wasn't very much we wanted to do. It was such a lazy day, and not even our folks wanted us to work in the garden, mow the lawn, or pick strawberries—things a boy gets to do on weekdays. So we ambled along toward the spring. Little Jim whammed away at different kinds of weeds with his stick as we went.

At the spring, the leaning linden tree didn't have a single bee swimming around among its creamy yellow flowers, because there weren't any flowers anymore. They had changed into smallish nuts the shape of Mom's Alderman peas, only a lot smaller. So what used to be thousands of sweet-smelling flowers were now flower seeds, each cluster hanging from the center of a long narrow leaf, which wasn't a *leaf,* John Fenwick had taught us, but was a *bract* and was the Lord's way of making new linden trees.

"In the fall, the sail-like leaf lets go from the tree that gave it birth and takes off in the wind to some hiding place where it lets nature bury it under a leaf or beside a fallen log. And by and by you have another linden tree."

We had learned a lot of things like that, most of which John had read to us out of the manuscript of a book he was writing.

As we sort of dreamed along toward the Collins house, it seemed that God was everywhere, breaking the bread of life and feeding the hungry world with Bible truth. He was also feeding His nature world all the time with rain and sunshine and reseeding it. It seemed a shame that when the Savior was here, His enemies hated Him enough to drive nails into His hands and feet. It just didn't seem right to hate anybody—not even anybody!

And then the Fenwicks' time in Maple Leaf was about over, and only a little more than a week was left.

The gang had another get-together one lazy afternoon—an afternoon so hot we had to go in swimming.

As soon as we were through swimming and diving and water fighting and were under the Snatzerpazooka tree dressing, we heard the sound of the *Vida Eterna* coming from up the creek in the direction of Shorty Long's place.

We quickly looked toward the east, expecting to see a man in a boat with a chubby boy in the stern driving, but instead it was John alone. He had come from his favorite fishing place upstream and had two of the biggest bass I had ever seen, except for Old Whopper himself, who was maybe five inches longer and a lot bigger around.

"What k–kind of bait did you use?" Dragonfly wanted to know.

John surprised us. "A dead minnow!"

I felt skeptical because any boy knows a bass will bite on live minnows but not on dead ones.

Still sitting in the boat, its prow resting on the sandy shore, John opened his new three-drawer tackle box and showed us what he called his "injured minnow." It looked exactly like a live minnow, but it had a three-barbed hook dangling from its tail and another from one side. It also had a shining spinner at its mouth where it was attached to a six-inch leader.

I had my eyes on about thirteen other artificial lures lying in separate compartments in the tackle box, and I thought how I'd like to have a box like that and a lot of fancy lures.

"Want to see how it works?" John asked us. When we said we did, he quickly attached the leader to his fishing line and dropped the minnow into the water at the edge of the boat. Instead of sinking, the live-looking "dead" minnow rolled over on its side and lay like flotsam on the surface. One of its artificial eyes was above the water and the other under, looking for all the world like an honest-to-goodness chub, the kind we catch in our seine in the fast water under the branch bridge.

"Now," John said to us, "if you yourself were a fish hiding down under the water somewhere, very hungry, and waiting for breakfast, dinner, or supper to come swimming past, and all of a sudden, out of a clear sky, a minnow like this came splashing down like it had fallen from a tree, wouldn't you think your supper was being handed to you on a silver platter?"

"Old Whopper wouldn't think that!" Little Jim said proudly. "He'd know minnows don't grow on trees. He'd maybe race out to take a look at it, but he'd just give his tail a disgusted flip, turn around, and swim back to bed."

"All right," John said, "let's find out what

little old 'injured minnow' here can do. See that stump in the water away over there on the other side? I'll risk a guess there's a bass or two, hungry for dinner even in the afternoon, when bass generally are too lazy to bite."

With that, John turned, gave his shining casting rod a swing, and Old Injured sailed out across our swimming hole and landed with a splash about two feet from the stump. Then John began to whisper under his breath, counting, "One, two, three . . ." while the "injured minnow" lay right there in the center of the little splash it had made when it struck the water.

"Twenty-one, twenty-two . . ."

At the count of thirty, John gave the tip of his rod a little flip. And away out near the stump, the minnow made a small splash on the surface.

Twice John counted to thirty, giving a quick flick of his wrist each time. And then something startling happened. There was a splash, a double splash, and, like lightning on the end of a fishing line—thunder and lightning and a tornado—a bass shot up into the air, shaking his shining body furiously, trying to throw the injured minnow out of his mouth, and not being able to. And in less time than it would take me to write all of it, John Fenwick had landed a whopper of a smallmouth bass!

There was a lot of excitement around that boat while he was reeling in the medium-sized whopper and while the bass was still fighting against being caught. In the middle of all the action, the closed tackle box got in the way.

And before we knew what was happening, it was off the boat seat and into the water.

I lunged for it and missed, but I needn't have worried. It had fallen onto its side and—like the salt and pepper shakers on our table at home, which won't stay on their sides when you accidentally tumble them over but are quickly upright again—that new, shining tackle box was upright and floating.

"Never have to worry about losing it in an upset," John told us. "A friend of ours in Pennsylvania gave it to us for Christmas last year when he learned we were going to have an enforced furlough."

I set the tackle box back on the boat seat and made sure the catch was fastened, glad for John that it hadn't been *open* when it fell into the water, or we would have had to search all over the creek bottom for the maybe thirteen lures the three trays had in them.

Little Jim, wide-eyed at what had been going on, glad we had caught such a big fish, and also feeling sorry for the fish because it got caught, all of a sudden pointed with his stick toward something floating out in the center of our swimming hole. He exclaimed, "Look! There's another big fish, floating like it was dead!"

We all looked where Little Jim was pointing, and, sure enough, there *was* a fish. Its body was swollen as if it had maybe been dead for quite a while. It was drifting along with the current.

That's when John Fenwick, still a missionary in spite of being on furlough, taught us a very important lesson, which was as good as any sermon our pastor had ever preached. He said, "Every boy in the world can take his choice of what kind of life he wants to live. Always remember this—something my own father once taught me—any old dead fish can float downstream. It's the live fish that swim upstream."

While big John was talking, he had a small fire in his eye that made me proud to be his friend. And I could almost hear myself thinking to myself and saying, *Bill Collins, what kind of boy are you going to be in life? Are you going to be any old dead fish, or are you going to be alive? You can take your choice.*

In a few minutes John would be on his way back to the Maple Leaf, where Elona would be waiting. And she would hurry down to the dock to help him beach the boat—not wanting him, because of his heart, to drag the *Vida Eterna* up onto the sand.

I was surprised to hear myself saying something else to myself right then, and it was, *I'm making my choice right now.* My jaw and my mind were set as I said it.

"Want to ride down to the Maple Leaf with me?" John asked us.

Dragonfly said, "Sure!"

The rest of us thought the same thing, and some of us said so.

And as soon as the bass was safe in the net with the other two, we pushed farther out from shore to where the water was deep enough for the propeller to work. In a few seconds there was a roar as the starter cord of the motor did what a starter cord is supposed to do. And away we went putt-putting downstream, the wind in our faces, our shirt sleeves flapping, and the shoreline drifting past as we skimmed happily along.

I was sitting in the seat just ahead of John, riding backward, when he surprised me with, "Want to steer it?"

Did I want to steer it! There was nothing I wanted to do more.

John adjusted the throttle so that we would be going only as fast as a boy rowing slowly. He and I changed seats, and I myself, Bill Collins, Theodore Collins's first and worst and only son, was the captain of the *Vida Eterna,* riding down Sugar Creek. My crew of six sailors was sitting in the seats in front of me, the prow of my vessel was raised a little, and the waves were parting like deep snow being hit by a snow-plow. Behind us the water was churning in the wake of my ship, which right then, when John told me to move the throttle to the left, leaped into life and began racing downstream maybe twice as fast as it had been.

In almost no time we passed the spring and somebody's old flat-bottomed, homemade, unpainted boat chained to a small maple sapling there. And then we were out in the middle of the creek, headed for the bridge.

It seemed all ten eyes of five of my crew were looking at me with envy, but I couldn't be bothered. I was the captain, and they were only the crew.

It was Little Jim who brought me back to Sugar Creek right then when he yelled, "Look out! You're going to smash into the big rock!"

And I did look out, by shoving the steering handle of the outboard to the left. That is, that was what I thought I was doing. Instead, I must have opened the throttle, because the *Vida Eterna* came to furious life and headed straight for the rock. It looked like a big gray-white freight car rushing toward me.

How we missed that monster rock I didn't know until afterward: Then I remembered, as we went sailing safely past, that John had quickly leaned over and shoved the steering handle in the right direction. We made a sharp, sideways turn and roared across the roof of Old Whopper's house like a jet zooming over the tops of the twin pignut trees—missing the big rock by only a few feet.

I wasn't very proud of myself as I kept the throttle where it belonged and, as John guided me with his voice, steered past the mouth of the branch, made a wide, slow circle, and nosed the *Vida Eterna* up to the sandy beach beside the Maple Leaf dock.

John shut off the motor so that we could glide in instead of racing in and hitting the shore or the dock with a *wham.*

Elona came out of the cabin and called us to come on up for a snack. As I climbed kind of slowly up the winding path to the outdoor fireplace, I noticed there was a bed of live coals and a pot of coffee on the grate, as if she had been expecting her husband and was waiting for him the way Mom had been waiting for Dad that night in the moonlight by the plum tree.

Soon John was sitting in his big lawn chair drinking his coffee, and the gang was drinking a cool drink of what you already know Elona called Costa Rican punch. All of a sudden the missionary caught at his chest, dropped his cup, leaned forward, and began to breathe hard, as if he had just landed a big fish and had had too much excitement bringing it to net.

Like a streak of flurrying green lightning, which was the color of Elona Fenwick's clothes, she was across the open space to him and searching in his shirt pocket for something. She brought out a small brown bottle, took out a tablet of some kind, and slipped it under John's tongue.

She was panting as hard as he was, and there was a worried expression on her face as well as on his.

Turning to us, she said, "He'll be all right in a minute. That's why we're here in the States instead of in Central America. John's heart has been on the warpath, so we have to be very careful. As long as we keep watching, and he keeps his nitroglycerin tablets handy, he'll be all right."

But the worry on her face showed it was not all right in her mind. She was afraid for her husband—afraid, maybe, that he might not always have his pills with him or might not be able to take one quickly enough.

But in a little while John was breathing as normally as any of us, and we finished our visit. We asked if there was anything we could do around the place. There was, and we did it, and then we went on home.

I was still a little proud of myself that I had been such a good captain of the boat for a while, even though I was remembering something my smart father had once said. And as I opened the gate near "Theodore Collins" on our mailbox, I was repeating it to myself. *"There are two kinds of proud."*

Charlotte Ann came racing out to meet me, bringing Elsie Jo with her. Her bare feet went plop-plopping in the dust of the road.

"How do you do, my friend?" I said down to her, hoping she wouldn't expect me to swoop her up and carry her into the house, as she sometimes does. I couldn't swoop her up when she was wearing a nice clean dress like that and while my hands were still smelling of fish from having helped John Fenwick take the three bass out of the net just before we left.

Charlotte Ann's mind was not on her big brother, however, but on Elsie Jo, who was thirsty again. I watched her lay her pink-dressed doll carefully on the edge of the water trough, then pumped myself a pan of water and carried it to the grape-arbor table to wash my hands, while Charlotte Ann filled Elsie Jo's bottle.

Even as I was drying my hands on the roller

towel, I noticed my weatherworn cane fishing pole leaning against the crossbeam and, wrapped round and round its long yellowish length, my two-year-old fishing line. On the end of the line were a metal sinker, a wire leader, and a single hook on which, when I went fishing, I had to use ordinary fishing worms I myself had to dig. It seemed the captain of the boat ought to have a box full of shining lures that could fool a smart bass into striking even in the daytime when ordinarily a bass should be taking an afternoon nap.

I didn't have even a floating tackle box in which to keep my lures, which I didn't have anyway.

I was wallowing around in the middle of my misery about the captain of the boat not having good fishing equipment, when from behind me I heard a little girl scream as if her world was coming to an end.

"Bill! Quick! Elsie Jo's drowning! Quick!"

7

That was one of the nicest things about being a brother. I had a chance to watch a little sister grow up, even though she was growing too slowly. By the time she would be old enough to be any help to Mom with the dishes, I would be almost too old to keep on helping—or I hoped I would be too old, anyway.

I really needn't have worried about ever getting too old, though, because my own father—who, it seemed, ought to know better—would sometimes make Mom go into the living room and rest in our easy chair, while he and his young son cleaned up the kitchen.

As I said, that was one of the nicest things about being the brother of a small sister. I got a chance to find out what puzzling people little girls are, too. Honestly, you never saw such an interesting human being, which Charlotte Ann was most of the time. She could be doing one thing and thinking about something else maybe a mile away. Sometimes you would see her looking into Mom's hand mirror in the downstairs bedroom as though she was an insect looking into an ant lion's nest under the walnut tree, trying to decide whether it would be safe to tumble into it.

Once I saw her out in the barnyard lying on

her dolly blanket, watching the swallows darting around in the late afternoon sky. They were catching moths and other flying things, and she was humming a little tune about brightening the corner where you are. Elsie Jo was resting on her arm at the time, and, when I accidentally happened along, Charlotte Ann shushed me, saying, "*Sh!* She's been counting the swallows, and it's making her sleepy."

Imagine that! Counting swallows, when anybody knows it's sheep you are supposed to count when you are trying to make yourself sleepy!

Another time, when she was kneeling at her bedside to say a good-night prayer to God, she finished her little memorized prayer and added, "And please keep watch over Elsie Jo tonight. She's afraid of the dark."

I was about to tiptoe out of the room when my neat little sister stopped me, saying, "She's still afraid of the dark, so leave the light on in the hall."

Just to help Elsie feel a little more safe, I gave her a little pat on her brown wavy hair and said, "It's all right, Elsie Jo, your mother's right here. She'll take care of you. You just call her if you're afraid or want a drink of water or anything—"

I didn't get to finish my advice to Elsie because Charlotte Ann cut in to say, "She's thirsty *now.*"

I said to myself as I went out to the pump for a fresh drink for a doll and her mother,

When, Bill Collins, will you learn not to put ideas into a doll's head?

After the water, I had to read Elsie a bedtime story about a little dragonfly, the kind that is called a darning needle dragonfly. Everywhere it flew down along the creek or when it was skimming over the surface of the muskrat pond in the swamp, it would say with its widespread buzzing wings, *"Be kind! Be kind!"* Then the big green darner would spot a mosquito, make a dive for it, and gobble it up—not being kind to the mosquito but only to boys, which mosquitoes are always unkind to.

"The green darning needle dragonfly," I said to Charlotte Ann's heavy eyelids, while Elsie Jo's eyes were already closed, "is supposed to watch when a boy plays hooky from school. And when it gets a chance, it comes in for a quick landing like an airplane, lights on the boy's ears, and sews them up tight. But it never, never sews up a little girl's ears . . ."

I knew it was only a story people tell about the Aeshnid dragonfly, and everybody knows it's not a true story but only a tale children like to hear, and it doesn't hurt them to hear it—if their ears haven't been sewed up yet.

Anyway, this past year especially, I had come to realize that Elsie Jo was a real person in my cute little sister's mind and not just a cuddly doll. So while I was standing by the grape arbor drying my hands—and in my mind was out in the boat and the captain of it—and my sister screamed for me to "come quick! Elsie Jo's drowning!" for a second, I was actually scared myself.

Like a boy making a reverse turn in a basketball game, I whirled, made a dash to the water trough on the other side of the pump, reached in, scooped up Elsie Jo, shook the water off her soaking-wet pink dress, and handed her to Charlotte Ann.

"There you are—all safe and sound."

But in Charlotte Ann's mind, that dripping wet, real live doll wasn't safe, and she wasn't sound. Not yet.

There were tears in Charlotte Ann's voice and actual ones in her eyes as she sobbed, *"She's drowned! You have to call the fire department!"*

Now where in the world did she get an idea like that? How did she know about calling the fire department? Then I remembered the true story of the little boy over in Brown County who had nearly drowned in a bathtub, and the fire department had come and revived him. Dad had read it to us from the paper.

"OK," I said, "you keep her warm."

I dashed to the grape arbor, picked up an imaginary phone like the one we have by the east window of our living room, and called an imaginary fire department. Then, making my voice sound like a siren and a fire engine motor, I came charging in from town. Then I—an imaginary fireman who knew all about first aid for drowning people—stretched little Elsie Jo out on her doll blanket on the pump platform.

It was going to be as easy as eating one of Mom's hot rolls to revive Elsie Jo. Before beginning, I looked across to Charlotte Ann's serious face and asked, "How old is she? Is she under three or over?"

My little sister held up three fingers, which was how old she herself was. So I began to give Elsie mouth-to-mouth resuscitation. I could have given her mouth-to-nose respiration, which is also a good way, but she didn't have any open nostrils.

I could feel Charlotte's worried eye watching me, so I kept a straight face, not blowing hard into Elsie Jo's imaginary lungs but using puffs of air from my cheeks, which is what you do for a child under three years of age. Elsie was actually only two.

In almost no time, the victim of the water trough drowning was breathing, maybe even better than she had been when she was alive. I was giving a sixth or seventh puff from my cheeks when Elsie Jo's mother stopped me, saying crossly, "Stop! She's already saved, and she has to put on a dry dress!"

While I was back again at the grape arbor, still thinking about the captain of the boat needing a new tackle box, my small sister was looking after her alive-again doll. And almost before I could get my hands dry on the roller towel, she was out in the barnyard wheeling her baby around like an old mother hen with one tiny baby chicken.

Even though it had only been an imaginary

lifesaving experience, I did feel proud of myself in the right way that I had had good self-control and had remembered especially about using only cheek puffs for children under three.

I might never in all my life have to give a real person artificial respiration, but it felt good to know that, if I ever did have to, I would know all the rules.

Three days later, just one week before the Fenwicks' time in the cabin would be up and they would move to Colorado where John would be a "missionary in residence" and teach missions in a seminary, the gang had a get-together at the Black Widow Stump. In another month, our wonderful summer would be over, and we would be back in school again.

As we do sometimes when we are together, we stretched out on our backs on the ground in what we called our wagon-wheel business meeting. That meant all our heads would be close together, making the hub of the wheel, and our feet would be stretched out in six directions—our legs spread a little so that we would make twelve different-length spokes instead of just six.

There wasn't any rim on our wheel, but that didn't matter, just so we had a good hub. That way we could hear each other without having to say, "What?"

Big Jim opened the meeting. "Well, gang, we learned a lot this summer—"

But that was as far as he got, because Little

Jim cut in with, "We're getting to be smart like the birds. The robins, the catbirds, the bluebirds, thrushes, and even the crows build their nests in the same woods, like my mother says."

That started all the spokes to talking, and when we had finished our ideas—some of which didn't amount to much—Big Jim came out with some pretty good boy wisdom when he said, "We have learned that one of the best rules of life is to live and *help* live, not just live and *let* live. We've found there is enough water in the creek for two boats, enough fish for everybody, enough air to breathe, and that the same birds sing for everybody—"

I couldn't resist putting in a kind of ornery thought right then, and it was, "But there are *not* enough groundhogs for everybody to shoot!"

I was surprised that there was as much fire in my voice as there was, and I didn't realize that some of the gang's tempers against Shorty Long were still as tinderbox-like as mine. In seconds we had unrolled ourselves from ourselves and were talking like a flock of blackbirds getting ready to fly South for the winter.

Big Jim took command of our boat then, saying, "All right, now. Everybody!" He raised his voice. "We don't hate Shorty Long! Is that clear?"

And it was.

"Next week, the white boat will be gone. We'll have to get used to using our own, and *we're not ashamed of ours.* Is that clear?"

And it was.

"And now," Big Jim ordered us, not bothering to ask anybody if anybody wanted to do it, "we're going to get our own boat ready for use. We're going to wash it, drag it up on the shore, paint it, build some Styrofoam into the seats, and be proud of it. Is *that* clear?"

And it was.

First we went down the incline to the spring to get a drink. There was not a single honeybee interested in the small, brown, nutlike seeds hanging from the middle of a bract.

Pretty soon we had all had a drink, kneeling down and drinking like cows. Then the gang started toward where we had our boat chained to its maple sapling.

Little Jim and I stayed behind for a while, because he had a secret he wanted to tell me. It was, "We're going to get a new baby at our house—a little brother."

We were standing near the Black Widow Stump at the time, and Chippy-chip-chee was acting the way a chipmunk acts when it is half afraid of you but is begging for anything you might have to offer.

"A little girl baby would be better, if she was as nice as Charlotte Ann," I suggested.

Little Jim stooped, held out his hand to Chippy-chip-chee, called him to come, then tossed a peanut toward the stump. And Chippy took off after it, getting to it and scooping it up in his paws just as I said, "We might get a baby brother at our house too!"

Big Jim called us then, and we went on the run to catch up with the rest of the gang and to help them drag the boat up onto the beach.

Even as I ran, I didn't have any idea why I had just said that to Little Jim, but it seemed like a good idea. It would be good for Charlotte Ann to have a little brother to play with and to share her toys with. We hadn't had a new baby at our house for more than three years.

We pulled the boat up on the sand and left it upside down in the sun to dry, which it would have to do before we could paint it. Besides, we didn't have the paint for it yet.

Then we went back to the spring, filled several glass jugs with water, and started to take them to the Maple Leaf, thinking that Elona maybe needed fresh springwater for making Costa Rican punch for anybody who might like to drink some.

Before starting to cross the bridge, Poetry and I stopped to pick up a few stones and sticks to throw down the creek near the big rock—just to see if Old Whopper was still there and all right and hadn't been fooled by some fancy lure into getting himself hooked and into somebody's frying pan.

We tossed rock after rock and stick after stick, scaring the turtles into scrambling for safety into their underwater hideaways, and not even once did Old Whopper bother to dash out to see what was going on.

"He's getting lazy," Little Jim suggested.

Big Jim solved the problem by reminding us in a teacher voice, "In the middle of the afternoon, bass are sleepy. Remember?"

And with that, Poetry raised his own voice in a teacher tone, announcing, "Class is dismissed!"

I quickly looked at Big Jim's lowered eyebrows as he reminded us, "We agreed, didn't we, back there at the stump that we *don't* hate Shorty Long!"

And it was clear again.

"Listen," Dragonfly exclaimed. "Here comes the *Vida Eterna!*"

Looking upstream in the direction of the spring, our swimming hole, and on farther toward where Shorty Long lived, I saw a flash of sunlight glancing from the white boat.

In a little while the boat reached the narrows below the swimming hole, where the water was too shallow for the motor's propeller. There the driver shut it off, and I could see that whoever was in the boat was using the oars for a while until he would reach deeper water.

Then the motor started again. In a little while, big John Fenwick's voice would be singing a song he nearly always sang when he was coming in for a landing at the Maple Leaf dock: "Sailing, sailing, over the bounding main . . ." And away down at the Maple Leaf, Elona would hear the song and come hurrying out and down to the dock to meet him.

Only a few more days and we'd maybe never again get to hear his booming voice singing and never again get to see Elona hurrying out to help him beach the boat.

Just then something happened! The motor came to startling roaring life just as if it was at full throttle. And the *Vida Eterna* came zooming toward us—faster and faster and still faster.

"Shorty Long!" a chorus of voices all around me called. "He's all alone!"

It had to be Shorty. Maybe he was taking a last, fast, mad ride before having to give up the ship. John Fenwick himself would never drive the boat that fast. He would be more thoughtful of the underwater wildlife, not wanting to scare the sunfish, bluegills, bass, goggle-eyes, suckers, and other peace-loving fish half out of their fish wits.

But the boat was near enough now for me to see who was in it—and it was *not* Shorty Long. It was John Fenwick himself! He was leaning forward, his left hand on the steering handle of the outboard motor, his right hand on his chest, and he was *not* singing. He was calling, "Elona! Elona! Elona!"

I felt a creeping in my spine, and my heart pounded with fear. Something was wrong. Terribly, terribly wrong!

On and on and still on, nearer and nearer, the white boat thundered toward us. It shot under the bridge below us and out on the other side. And all the time, John was calling his wife's name as though he wanted her to know he was coming and to be ready for something terrible that was about to happen.

All of us scrambled to the other side of the bridge, watching the boat go flying toward the Maple Leaf.

And that's when the something I was afraid was going to happen *did* happen. John Fenwick slipped forward and sideways in the boat. His heavy body, with muscles as strong as iron bands, slumped over against the gunwale. At the same time, his left hand let go the steering handle.

The boat swerved toward the right and headed straight for the big rock, where two or three turtles had decided their world hadn't come to an end after all and were starting to crawl back onto their sundeck.

It was Big Jim who first guessed out loud what was happening. "A heart attack! He's having a heart attack!"

Dragonfly began to stammer out something or other. But before he could even get his idea started, the wild-running boat was in the middle of its accident. Its shining prow with *Vida Eterna* on it crashed head-on into the big rock. Then it lifted, shot up over it, and came down with a boiling of waves and scraping of its metal sides against the rock as the turtles turned turtle and shot back into their shelter again.

I saw the boat's life preserver fly into the air and land about fifteen feet away. The tackle box flew also, and they both started jouncing along on the widening waves.

John Fenwick himself was tossed out into

the deep water about ten feet from Old Whopper's hiding place. As he went down, he called out in a gasping, terrified voice, *"Elona! Elona!"*

And now all my warm feeling for big John Fenwick melted my whole heart, and I started thinking about Elona. Her husband might be dying, and she would be left alone in the world without her John, as all alone and brokenhearted as my own mother would be without Dad.

But I was daydreaming when I should have been *doing* something. There was a flurry of action now beside me, and the sound of a boy's bare feet on the wooden bridge. I quick looked, and there was Circus, the fastest runner of all of us, flying like a curly-headed arrow for the other end of the bridge, calling over his shoulder to us, "Come on, gang! Let's go save him!"

8

And now there were twelve flying feet racing for the north end of the long bridge. Twelve plop-plopping feet and six minds, all of us thinking and worrying and planning and hoping, wondering how we were going to help, and if we *could* help, and what if we couldn't!

As I ran, my feet seemed to drag like lead, the way they do sometimes in a dream when I am trying to get away from something or somebody and can't.

Down the steep embankment on the other side, through the thicket of shrubbery that sheltered the shore, at last we broke out into the open space on the beach itself. I saw the aluminum boat, upright again like a weighted saltshaker and empty except for the water that was in it. Already it had floated downstream a ways, and beside it was the life preserver, like a baby chicken staying close to its mother in a time of danger.

The tackle box and the oars weren't anywhere in sight, and neither was big John Fenwick. My mind told me the terrible truth—John had had a heart attack, and, even though he was a good swimmer, he hadn't been able to swim a stroke! He was already drowned!

All the things John had taught us about lifesaving seemed to jam up in my mind. This wasn't any Elsie Jo rescue, where all you had to do was reach into a water tank, pull the doll out, and give her mouth-to-mouth artificial respiration until your kid sister decided her doll was alive again.

But the different methods of water rescue *were* in my mind, piled up like driftwood on the Sugar Creek island during a spring flood:

Reaching rescue was out, because there wasn't a thing to reach out to John with—no branches or sticks or paddles or bath towels or anything. Besides, there wasn't anybody to reach them *to!*

Throwing rescue couldn't even be considered, because how could we throw a life preserver when the only one in Sugar Creek was by now sixty yards downstream?

Boat rescue was already too late. The only boat anywhere nearby *wasn't* near and was drifting farther away each second. The only other boat was upstream farther than that!

The *floating device rescue* method was also no good, because we didn't have an air mattress or anything to float out to him on . . .

All four plans were out, simply *out!*

Reach—Throw—Row—Go. These were the four best methods of rescue for a drowning person, and not a one of them would work. Not even the *Go* method, because where could we go?

If John was already drowned, then all that would be left would be an underwater search for the body. If we found it, we could bring it to the surface and to the shore. And if he *was* still alive, or even if he seemed to be dead, we could try artificial respiration.

There was *only* one thing left to do, and I was going to do it. For a minute it seemed I was the only member of the gang there. I could get my clothes off in less than ten seconds flat and be stripped to my shorts. I could go rushing out through the shallow water toward the big rock and make a dive underwater there to see if I could find John Fenwick down there somewhere.

But I guess I wasn't really using my head. I was already half out of my clothes when Big Jim's captainlike voice stopped me. "Bill," he shouted, "you run home and telephone the fire department, and maybe your dad can come and help. Get your mother on the phone for all the Sugar Creek dads. Poetry, you and Dragonfly go down and tell Elona to pray. And Little Jim, you stay here with Circus and me. We'll search for his body and bring it in and start artificial respiration. And, listen, everybody! *Everybody pray on the run! Run and pray and work!* We're the only guys God has right now to save the life of one of the best friends He ever had! Go on, Bill! Get going!"

And I got going! My clothes were back on in seconds. Big Jim's thundering orders were like strong hands helping me dress.

Back through the dense thicket I worked my way. Up the steep incline to the bridge I raced, panting, hurrying, worrying, thinking, hoping—and praying. I seemed to be the only boy the Lord had at the time to do what I had to do. I was helping Him, and He was helping me.

I was halfway across the long bridge—hoping any second I would meet a car or see somebody I could stop and tell what was happening down by the big rock—when I got a feeling in my mind that I ought to look back downstream.

I didn't stop running but looked on the run. By the shore I saw Big Jim and Circus, already stripped to their shorts, beginning to wade toward where we'd last seen John alive.

Little Jim was on the beach, still dressed, his ash stick in his hands, and I knew he was thinking that if John *was* still alive and he could reach out his cane to him, he would use all the strength his smallish muscles had to help pull him in.

I was still running and was almost to the other end of the bridge, when something else I had seen came into my mind. I stopped like a car having its four-wheel brakes slammed on and looked back. The wind or something had turned the boat so that its prow was headed upstream. And on the side next to the mouth of the branch, close to the boat and floating, I saw what looked like the body of a man.

In that second I knew John's body was *not* somewhere up near the big rock, deep down in Old Whopper's home territory, but that he had already drowned and had come to the surface and was floating on his back alongside the boat, the way drowned bodies sometimes do.

I quickly let loose a wild yell to Big Jim and

Circus and Little Jim and to anybody else who could hear me. "Hey! Big Jim! Circus! Everybody! I see him! He's floating with the boat—*on the other side of it!*"

Circus and Big Jim had been spared a long underwater search for the body. Now they could go racing down to the Maple Leaf dock, swim out, drag John's body to shore, and maybe even get him revived.

But if they couldn't, maybe the fire department could.

At a time like that, you don't have time to stop and listen to all the happy birds singing in the trees along the roadside or to the angry birds scolding if you happen to scare them off their nests. You just run and run and run and pant and hope and pray and keep on running and dodging briars and shrubbery and brush piles. The shortest way home was through the woods, and I was taking it.

The long, green, flat leaves of the papaw bushes hung like lazy half-closed umbrellas that didn't have a care in the world and had nothing to do but shade the papaw fruit from the hot sun. The wood thrush, when I went charging past her nest, broke out into a mad *"Prut-prut-prut!"* Even as I swished past, I called out to her, "You don't need to lose your temper over anything! You've already hatched your eggs, and your thrush babies have learned to fly already."

On and still on. *Fire department. Fire department. Fire department. Maybe the fire department can help.*

I was getting close to the Black Widow Stump, where I would make the last turn before flying up the long slope to our house, when Chippy-chip-chee, who had been taking his afternoon nap, reared up in a quick freeze. Then, when I didn't stop, he dropped out of sight on the other side.

That's when I saw and heard somebody coming from the direction of the swimming hole and the bayou. It was a big boy, panting and running and crying—actually crying! It was Shorty Long, and he was soaking wet!

"John! Uncle John!" he was calling. "I found your pills! I found your pills!"

I stopped and yelled to Shorty, "What on earth?"

But all I got out of him was a mumbled "We caught a bass out in front of our dock. I fell out of the boat, and he reached for me and dropped his pills in the water. We couldn't find 'em. He was racing home to get some more. I saw his boat hit the big rock."

And then, as Shorty swung into a sobbing, soaking, splashety run for the bridge, and as I swerved south toward our house, I thought I heard him crying out something else. Exactly what, I didn't know, but part of it sounded like "Please, God, help me get there in time."

As I charged up the slope, it seemed I was doing and saying the same thing my enemy was —crying and praying, "Please, God, help me to get there in time!"

Every step I took, my mind's eye was seeing

one of the worst boys who had ever lived in Sugar Creek territory, running and praying and hoping, carrying with him a little bottle of lifesaving pills. And I was glad that I hadn't told Shorty it was already too late, that big John Fenwick was already drowned and his body was floating alongside the *Vida Eterna.*

It just didn't seem right—a kind, wonderful man such as John, who had given his life in Central America to preach and teach the only gospel there ever was to people who would be lost without it—having to die when he wasn't any older than my father. A man like John ought to live forever.

I was at the elderberry bushes now, where once, a long time ago, which also seemed like yesterday, two boys had had a fistfight, and a hot-word fight. As I went flying over the rail fence and scooting across the dusty road to "Theodore Collins" on our mailbox, I heard a song in my mind. It was: *"Yo tengo vida eterna en mi corazon."* And I knew that no matter what happened to John's body, after the muscles that had been as strong as iron bands were buried somewhere, his soul had eternal life and *would* live forever!

I gulped and shot through the gate, leaving it open so that, when I came back from phoning the fire department, I could fly through and be on my way to the Maple Leaf to do anything I could to help Big Jim and Circus.

I was surprised that Charlotte Ann didn't come racing across the yard to meet me, wanting to be lifted and carried into the house. She nearly always does that when it is Dad coming home, and she was beginning to try to get me to do the same thing.

At the back screen door, there was a note from Mom fastened to the knob, which said:

> Bill, there has been an emergency, and I have gone to the hospital with Little Jim's mother. If I'm late for supper, help yourself to anything you can find. There is cold chicken and apple pie. Your father phoned that he will be late, too. I've taken Charlotte Ann, so you're the man of the house. Old Bent Comb is getting a little stubborn about going into the coop behind the grape arbor, so let her take her babies anywhere she wants to.

I couldn't be bothered with worrying about a choosy old setting hen and her chicks when there was an emergency that had to have the fire department.

I was surprised to find our party line not busy, so I quickly had Sam LaRue, the fire chief, on the phone. I told him what had happened and where, and he said not to worry—just do what we could—and he'd get Dr. Basset if *he* could and would bring the inhalator.

"Dr. Basset's at the hospital right now," Sam said to me, "but I'll get him. And the ambulance."

In almost no time I was out of the house,

racing across the yard, through the gate, and on my way to the Maple Leaf to tell everybody that help would soon be coming at seventy-five miles an hour.

I guess my heart had never had a bigger ache than it had right that minute as I flew, flew, flew through the woods, across the bridge, down the embankment, and along the narrow path to where the rest of the gang was. I was worrying about Elona, whose heart would be broken if John had really drowned and couldn't be revived.

She and their little foreign car were gone, I found out, and she had left a note on the dock post that said,

> Dear John, I've gone to the drugstore for a new supply of medicine. Did you realize you were out, and all we had was in the little bottle you carry with you?

Even as I saw what was going on, I thought it was better that Elona was *not* there in case—just in case—John could not be revived before his spirit had left his body for good.

The boat, I noticed, was out where it had been when I'd seen it from the bridge, still with its prow pointed upstream.

"The anchor got thrown out of the boat when it hit Old Whopper's rock," Little Jim explained, "and the boat floated this far before the anchor struck the bottom."

But it wasn't the boat or the anchor I was

interested in but what was happening on the beach beside the dock, where Big Jim and Circus were working over John's body. Big Jim himself was giving mouth-to-mouth respiration.

Shorty Long was there too, standing a few feet away, sniffling a little and begging them to let him help. "I know how to do it," he exclaimed. "Uncle John taught me how."

Big Jim had his ear close to John's open mouth now, listening to see if the air he had just blown into it and down into his lungs was coming back out. But it seemed it wasn't, because he kept on doing it—blowing in hard, then stopping to listen, doing it over and over again. It seemed we had never had a better captain of the ship than Big Jim or a better first mate than Circus. They were keeping their heads and working like doctors during an operation.

Big Jim looked up at us then and shook his head. "Nothing yet, but he's not dead. His heart is still beating."

While he was still speaking, I saw the fingers of John's right hand twitch. Then—even from as far away as I was—I heard a sighlike gasp.

Again Big Jim blew in a lungful of air, and again he listened. And this time for sure, something happened. There was the sound of air coming out. And I saw the short, sharp rise and fall of John Fenwick's chest as he began to breathe without help.

That's when the lesson we had passed the

examination on really came in handy, because John seemed to regain consciousness and want to sit up. But Big Jim and Circus held him down. They did let him have his head as high as a folded shirt for a pillow would raise it but no higher.

"A drowning victim can stop breathing again soon after he starts." That had been part of the lesson. "So watch every second, and be ready to start artificial respiration again."

We didn't even have time to relax, for in only a few minutes John's old heart trouble started again. He began to breathe fast and hard, and his face showed he was having a lot of pain.

Then there was the sound of shuffling feet in the sand beside me as Shorty Long hurried to where John was. He dropped onto his knees beside the man who had adopted him for the summer. He slipped a nitroglycerin tablet under John's tongue. And the life of one of the finest persons who had ever lived was saved.

And then there was the sound of car wheels on the board bridge and a siren and, behind the car, an ambulance.

Dr. Basset took charge the minute he was there, getting a cup of hot coffee into John and keeping him wrapped in a warm blanket until they could get him into the ambulance. They would watch over him all the way to the hospital, where they were going to take him for a few days for what is called "observation," just to be sure there wouldn't be a relapse.

Elona came driving in then, worried and scared when she saw all the people and her husband on the ambulance stretcher. But when Dr. Basset told her there'd been a little accident and her husband was all right, just needed hospital rest a few days, she dropped on her knees beside the stretcher and cried a little to John the way wives do to their husbands—anyway, as Mom does to Dad once in a while.

Dr. Basset turned now to look at Shorty Long and the rest of us, asking, "Which one of you is Jimmy Foote?"

Little Jim stood up proud at that and said, "I am." He said it kind of bashfully though.

"Well, I've just come from the hospital, and you have a beautiful, brand-new baby brother!"

You never in your life saw such a happy grin on a little guy's face. Little Jim quickly looked over at me and said, "What'd I tell you?"

Then he whirled and, spying a three-foot-tall milkweed stalk near the barbecue pit, he swung at it with a fierce, powerful swing as though the muscles of his slender arms were strong as iron bands. His stick knocked off a cluster of lilac-colored flowers and scared half out of its butterfly wits the monarch butterfly that had been sipping nectar there, sending it loping off across the open space between us and the Maple Leaf.

All of a sudden I was remembering not only what Little Jim had told me when we had been alone near the Black Widow Stump but also what I had told him. Then with my mind's eye I saw Mom's note on the kitchen door about an "emergency" and that she had gone to the hospital with Little Jim's mother. I quickly looked at Dr. Basset and said, "My name is Collins—Bill Collins."

Our family doctor looked at me with twinkling brown eyes. Then he said, "Oh, yes, I remember. You have a little sister. I helped bring her into the world, too!" He stopped, frowning as if trying to remember something.

I felt myself staring, getting topsy-turvy in my mind. "You mean . . ."

"I was just trying to recall her name. It's Charlotte Ann, I believe."

And that was that—a disappointing, mixed-up that, at that.

After the ambulance had taken John, and Elona with him, to the hospital, the gang was left alone to close the cottage, beach the boat, and be sure the fire in the barbecue pit was completely out.

Then we had to save another life—and right there in the same place, in front of the Maple Leaf dock.

9

After the ambulance had been gone maybe seven minutes, and the gang and Shorty Long were still at the dock feeling happy and sad at the same time, there was a problem in my mind.

"How," I asked Big Jim, "could his body float when it had just been drowned? I thought there would have to be a search for the body underwater. That's what we learned in Uncle John's lessons."

Circus had an answer ready. "Remember the fishnet he always drags alongside the boat? Well, he was trying to save himself from drowning—at least that's the way we figured it out—and his hand got tangled in it. Then he had his heart attack blackout and lost consciousness, but he floated because his hand was caught in the net."

It made sense, I thought, and wondered if, after John was 100 percent well and we could talk to him, he would remember all the things that had happened.

A saucy little wind came up right then, ruffling the water and turning the *Vida Eterna* this way and that. It was still anchored where it had been when I'd seen it from the bridge about an hour before. There was also a rumble of thunder like an automobile crossing the bridge.

"We'd better hurry up and get the boat beached," Big Jim said, "or the wind could whip her around against the dock and bang her up—or maybe blow her downstream to deeper water or all the way to the island. The anchor rope might even break."

"Let me go get her," I offered. I was quickly half out of my clothes, planning to swim out, pull up the anchor and row her in. Or, maybe —*maybe*—if the wind would blow a little harder, I'd have to start the motor and *drive* her in!

But it was an empty dream, which a certain poem says life is not. Instead, Circus and Big Jim, still in their shorts, *waded* out to the *Vida Eterna*. There wasn't going to be any need for the motor at all.

Circus had caught hold of the anchor rope and was starting to lift the anchor off the bottom when he let out a yell. "It's caught on something! There's something *alive* on it. It's pulling and jerking and trying to get away!"

What on earth? I thought. A crazy mixed-up idea flooded into my mind. There was a legend about a place at the bottom of the sea that is supposed to be the grave of all drowned persons. Some drowned person down there had hold of the anchor rope and wanted to be pulled out!

Big Jim knew what was happening, though. He told us, "The anchor, dragging along between here and the big rock, caught on Elona's trotline, and we've got a fish or two or more."

With that, he and Circus began to pull on

the anchor rope, dragging it and the boat toward the end of the dock, where I saw to it that I was in a hurry, ready to help and to get in on the excitement of seeing what we had caught.

In only a few half minutes more, the boat was all the way to the dock, and we were busy pulling in the trotline.

"Looks like we've caught the biggest catfish in the creek," Big Jim said, and I saw the muscles of his brawny arms and shoulders rippling like ropes as he dragged the trotline toward the side of the dock where the water was only two or three feet deep.

It looked like we were catching not only the biggest catfish there ever was but three or four of them, the way the line was slicing the surface of the water this way and that.

And then, out about fifteen feet from the stern of the *Vida Eterna* there was an explosion of the surface of the water like a volcano erupting in Davy Jones's locker. Up into the air shot the biggest bass any boy ever saw, shaking its body savagely and trying to get unhooked from one of Elona's trotline hooks.

"Old Whopper!" a half-dozen boys' voices cried. "We've caught Old Whopper!"

"He'll get himself killed!" Little Jim cried beside me.

"He'll tear his mouth out!" Poetry exclaimed. "We'd better *net* him."

And that is what we did do. Instead of playing Old Whopper the way you do an ordinary bass until he wears himself out or tears his mouth and gets away, we got John's landing net from the cabin. And, as soon as we had a chance, we had Old Whopper, gasping and as excited and wild-eyed as a pony somebody was trying to break to ride, in the center of the net. Big Jim held onto him with a damp cloth while Circus tried to carefully work the hook out of his mouth. But he couldn't. It wouldn't *come* out.

"Pliers," Big Jim said. "We need a pair of pliers. We can cut the shank and slide it out." The shank was the straight part of the hook.

"John's got a pair of pliers in the tackle box," Shorty Long said, beginning to look all around, even under the Styrofoam seats of the *Vida Eterna.*

But of course the box wasn't there. I had seen it floating away with the boat after the upset.

We had to keep Old Whopper wet or, even when we would let him loose, he might die. We all knew that if you catch a fish and don't plan to keep it and want it to live, you handle it with wet hands and you release it underwater. You never toss it back in—*never!*

But Dragonfly was using *his* head too. Everybody else was being a hero, and he and Little Jim hadn't had a chance to do anything important. All of a sudden, he called from down the shore, "Look, everybody! I found the tackle box!" It had lodged against a willow on the shore.

And so little spindle-legged, crooked-nosed, straight-muscled Dragonfly was a hero, too.

With the pliers from the box, Big Jim snipped off the hook. He eased it out of Old Whopper's mouth, and the biggest bass in Sugar Creek was free. The minute Old Whopper knew for sure he was free, he gave a disgusted flip of his tail, and took off for Davy Jones's locker or somewhere, as much as to say, "I didn't want those old fishing worms anyway! They're catfish bait! They're not fit for a fine fish like me!"

It had been a wonderful and a terrible day, not like any we had ever lived through in our whole lives.

The wind came to life then, harder than ever, and we knew that pretty soon, if seven boys didn't beat it for shelter, we'd get rained on.

It didn't seem to matter though. What was a little rainwater anyway?

In the climb to the Maple Leaf, Little Jim said to me secretly, "Every day's a wonderful day."

And it was.

Shorty was carrying the tackle box, and I heard him and Poetry talking as they puffed their chubby ways up the hill together.

I was surprised to hear Shorty say, "Aunt Elona is going to start a new club here in America. It'll be called the *Vida Eterna* Fishermen's Club, and I might become one of the charter members. As soon as any boy finds out in his heart what *vida eterna* means, he is already a member. And every new member is supposed to get *another* new member each year—or more, if he can."

A kind of happy thought came breezing into my mind right then. Big John Fenwick didn't have to live in a foreign country to be a missionary or a fisher of men. He had been fishing all summer, and he had caught a boy—a real whopper of a boy.

My thoughts were still a little mixed up, and I wasn't quite sure I *wanted* Shorty to stop being my enemy, because all my life it seemed I had had at least one. But it did feel good to have a warm heart toward anybody who was such a changed boy as Shorty seemed to be right then.

My tangled-up thoughts got straightened out in a hurry, though, when Shorty began to sing in a warbling falsetto the song Elona had taught us at our fish fries around the barbecue campfire and which we had heard the big fisherman from Costa Rica singing quite a few times when he was out in the boat alone. It was the one that begins, *"Yo tengo vida eterna en mi corazon."*

Shorty's voice didn't sound too bad. In fact, it sounded so good that Circus, the best singer of us all, stopped, looked back down the hill at Poetry and him huffing and puffing their way up, and called to Shorty, "With a voice like that I'll bet you could yodel."

I quickly looked at Circus, surprised at such a friendly tone of voice.

Then I had my attention blown away by a buzzing sound above my head, like a hummingbird darting around Mom's petunias.

Looking up, I saw not only *one* ruby-throated hummingbird buzzing around Elona's feeder but three green-backed, white-stomached, dark-winged, red-throated hummers, buzzing and chasing each other all around like a gang of boys having a rough-and-tumble good time around and over each other in Sugar Creek.

The humming and buzzing were like the humming and buzzing of a darning needle dragonfly, skimming along above the muskrat swamp, gobbling up mosquitoes, and droning his dragonfly song, *"Be kind. Be kind!"*

Little Jim, beside me, was trying to sing falsetto. *"Yo tengo vida eterna,"* he began, then stopped and said, "You know what my new brother's name is going to be?"

"No, what?" I asked.

And he answered with a grin. "*Littlest* Jim."

It wasn't a bad idea, I thought. And, when I studied his happy blue eyes looking up at me, I also thought, *There are two kinds of pride, and Little Jim has the best kind there is.*

There was a clap of thunder then, and when I took a look at the western sky, I saw old Long Neck Blue take off from the island and wing his way toward his favorite roosting place somewhere in the direction of the sycamore tree and the swamp.

From beside me, then, I heard Shorty Long's voice saying, "Here, Chippy! Here, little brother! Here's a peanut for you!"

I looked, and there was a neat little brown chipmunk the size and shape of Chippy-chip-chee, bashfully eyeing us from behind the barbecue pit, as though he wanted to be friends with anybody who had anything for him to eat.

There was a little glad feeling in my mind as I saw Shorty holding out his hand and saying, "Here's a peanut for you. It's a little wet, but it'll taste good."

And Chippy-chip-chee's brother—or cousin or uncle or maybe his father—scooted out, grabbed the wet peanut out of Shorty's hand, and away he went, a little brown streak of nature in a fur coat, happy to be living in a world where so many people were kind and nobody hated anybody.

Moody Press, a ministry of the Moody Bible Institute,
is designed for education, evangelization, and edification.
If we may assist you in knowing more about Christ
and the Christian life, please write us without obligation:
Moody Press, c/o MLM, Chicago, Illinois 60610.